KINGZ OF THE GAME 3

Lock Down Publications and Ca$h
Presents

Kingz of the Game 3
A Novel by *Playa Ray*

Lock Down Publications
P.O. Box 870494
Mesquite, Tx 75187

Visit our website @
www.lockdownpublications.com

Copyright 2019 Playa Ray
Kingz of the Game 3

First Edition August 2019
Printed in the United States of America

This is a work of fiction. Names, characters, places, and incidents either are products of the author's imagination or are used fictitiously. Any similarity to actual events or locales or persons, living or dead, is entirely coincidental.

Lock Down Publications
Like our page on Facebook: Lock Down Publications @
www.facebook.com/lockdownpublications.ldp
Cover design and layout by: **Dynasty Cover Me**
Book interior design by: **Shawn Walker**
Edited by: **Lashonda Johnson**

Stay Connected with Us!

Text **LOCKDOWN** to 22828 to stay up-to-date with new releases, sneak peaks, contests and more...

Thank you.

Submission Guideline.

Submit the first three chapters of your completed manuscript to ldpsubmissions@gmail.com, subject line: Your book's title. The manuscript must be in a .doc file and sent as an attachment. Document should be in Times New Roman, double spaced and in size 12 font. Also, provide your synopsis and full contact information. If sending multiple submissions, they must each be in a separate email.

Have a story but no way to send it electronically? You can still submit to LDP/Ca$h Presents. Send in the first three chapters, written or typed, of your completed manuscript to:

LDP: Submissions Dept
Po Box 870494
Mesquite, Tx 75187

DO NOT send original manuscript. Must be a duplicate.

Provide your synopsis and a cover letter containing your full contact information.

Thanks for considering LDP and Ca$h Presents.

ACKNOWLEDGMENTS

Y'all already know that God gets all the praise. Moreover, besides all of my supporters, I would like to give a huge shout out to all of my haters. No, I'm serious, if it wasn't for you, Playa Ray wouldn't even exist. Also, to the no-good women and fake friends, I've encountered along this life's journey. I really appreciate you all, you're the reason why I deal with people the way that I do now and why I go so hard with my writing.

However, being that success is the best revenge, I am more than willing to sweep your misdeeds under the rug and continue to reach for the stars. I mean, what's a raindrop to a river? Lock Down Publications has taken the game by storm, which automatically puts me on the winning team.

So, a big shout out goes out to Cash, Shawn Walker and the rest of the coaches and players at the LDP Publications division. Thanks for pulling me from the rubble and giving me a whole new look on life. Now, the world gets to find out who the real Playa Ray is.

Also, don't forget to shop DrogueClothing.com for the hottest gear on the planet!

"Greatness is not measured by what a man or woman accomplishes, but by the opposition, he or she has overcome to reach their goals."

Dorothy Height
American Civil Rights Activist (1912-2010)

Playa Ray

CHAPTER 1

Sheila was roused from her sleep by the sound of her cell phone sitting on the nightstand beside the alarm clock that by the digits displayed indicated she'd overslept and was late for work *again*. Therefore, she already knew who the call was from.

"Girl get your butt up!" Shonda demanded from the other end. "Don't tell me you over-slept again. Lieutenant Mallery is the shift's supervisor today. You know that bitch already don't like you. Are you coming in, or what?"

"I'm on my way out the door now," Sheila answered hating lying to her cousin.

"Well, hurry up!" Shonda told her. "They got me working with that stupid ass bitch, Price!"

Ending the call, Sheila quickly showered, donned her uniform, then exited the apartment, heading for her Kia Sportage that had become a huge liability in the last three months. It surprised her that the mid-sized SUV had started on the first try. Being that it was the second week of August. She rolled the windows down and enjoyed the cool morning breeze as she drove, listening to the *Frank Skee Morning Show*. She was enjoying the show until one of the hosts mentioned today was the twelfth of August. This caught Sheila off guard. She couldn't believe she'd let this day sneak up on her. This particular day marked one year since The Kingz were murdered.

At this time, Sheila couldn't parry the thoughts of that dreadful night. She remembered standing outside the club where the Battle of the D.J.s was being held, along with Shonda, Theresa, and Ebony. All day, she'd been rehearsing what she was going to say to Ray. She was not going to let him get away that night without him knowing how she really felt about him. But her plans were crushed when the club owner broadcasted that on his way to the club, he'd driven by the scene – which is why he was late – where The Kingz limousine had been riddled with bullets.

He was reluctant to assert that he'd witnessed The Kingz' lifeless bodies being extracted from the limousine and laid beside the truck for the Crime Scene Investigators to take pictures before covering them with the white sheets. The news hit her hard, but reality didn't kick in until she dropped Ebony and Theresa off, and she and Shonda returned home. She tried to be strong, but hearing Shonda cry her heart out in the next room, broke down her barrier, and she ended up crying herself to sleep.

When Sheila came to, she realized she was sitting in the parking lot of the Dekalb County Jail, with the engine still running. She rolled the windows up before shutting off the engine. After wiping the tears from her face and checking herself in the rearview mirror, she dismounted, heading for the building, ready to deal with Lieutenant Mallery.

"You're assigned to eight North-East, dorm two hundred," the tall, dark-skin lieutenant apprised Sheila, giving her a look that dared her to gripe about it.

Sheila knew better, she'd only been on the job for a little over five months and was already on the verge of losing it for being late for the fourth time in two months. Therefore, she gave Mallery a simple, 'Yes sir,' and headed for the elevators. If it wasn't for Shonda who'd helped her get the job, she may have given Mallery a piece of her mind and marched right back out the front door. She did not want to work on the eighth floor again, where they housed the inmates that were already sentenced and waiting to be transferred to prison with terms ranging from five years to life without parole.

Most of those guys, being that they were already sentenced, adopted the 'I don't care attitude', so there was always verbal and physical disputes. Plus, some of the inmates were very disrespectful to female officers and constantly making obscene comments and gestures. The last two times Sheila had worked on the floor, several guys pulled their penises out on her and masturbated. Therefore, they rarely sent female officers to the eighth floor.

"Kill on the floor!" some of the inmates yelled when Sheila entered the dorm and made for the booth that sat in the middle of the dorm, where two male officers, Grant and Lane, were stationed.

"Welcome back!" Grant greeted her, smiling.

Sheila was not going to entertain this dull wisecrack. At least Lane had enough sense not to say anything to her. Being that she was to relieve him, he grabbed his belongings and quickly made his exit. Sheila sat down in the chair beside Grant and did a once-over of the dorm. The inmates on the bottom range were out for their free time, watching TV, using the phones, or on the recreational yard, but all eyes were on her.

'They act like they ain't never seen a woman before,' she thought as she scribbled in the logbook.

"You okay?" Grant asked.

"Nope," she answered curtly, not lifting her eyes from the book.

"It's not that bad up here."

Now, she regarded Grant, who was 5'11, one-hundred and seventy pounds, dark-brown skinned, and looked as if he'd never missed a day at the gym. He had straight, white teeth, and dark wavy hair. Sheila considered him a pretty boy, and pretty boys were not her type. Plus, he had a reputation for sleeping with half of the women that worked at the jail.

"I mean, you'll stumble across a few knuckleheads," he continued, apparently not liking the look she was giving him. "Other than that, it's the same as the rest of the jail."

"It's punishment!" she contradicted.

"Only if you look at it that way."

Refusing to reply, Sheila picked up the desk phone and punched in four digits.

"Five South-East, dorm two hundred, Officer Price speaking."

"Is Officer Watson close by?" Sheila asked.

"Officer Watson," Shonda sounded on the other end.

"They got me on the eighth floor again," Sheila told her. "North-East, two hundred."

"I figured she was gonna do that," Shonda replied. "At least you're up there with Grant, with his fine ass!"

"Don't even go there!" Sheila protested, fighting the urge to look in his direction.

"I heard he got, at least, twelve inches between his legs," Shonda asserted, laughing.

"Shonda, I don't care about all that!" Sheila stated. "I'm not interested."

"Girl, please!" Shonda would not let up. "He can charm the panties off a mannequin!"

"Good for him!" Sheila finally cast a glance at Grant, who was looking in the opposite direction. "I called you for a reason, Shonda."

"What's that?"

"You know what today is?"

"Thursday."

"The date."

"The twelfth, what's so spec—"

Shonda was quiet on the other end. Apparently, she too had let today sneak up on her. The first and last time they'd been to The Kingz graves, was two weeks after they were buried. They didn't get to attend their funerals, because the services were not disclosed to the public. Shonda found out where The Kingz were buried, after running into DJ Spenz at a gas station. So, after conveying this information to Sheila, Ebony, and Theresa, they all bought flowers and dutifully paid their respects.

****

After getting off the phone with Sheila, all Shonda could think about was James and that dreadful night. She found herself in a somber mood for the rest of the day and was glad when the second shift relieving officers arrived.

Now, she was sitting in the jail's parking lot, in her red convertible Ford Mustang James had bought her, waiting for Sheila to exit the building. She would usually let her top down and relish the sun, after being cooped up inside that building for over eight hours. But today, she couldn't even bring herself to allow that pleasure.

Moments later, another group of officers exited the building. Shonda spotted Sheila as the group branched off, heading for their cars. Being that Shonda had parked her car in front of Sheila's, she was headed in her direction.

"You called, Ebony?" Sheila asked, approaching.

"Yeah," Shonda answered. "She wants us to meet her at the shop, around five o'clock."

"Are you bringing flowers?"

"If I can catch a florist before they close," she answered. "First, I gotta stop at an ATM. You got some money?"

"I should have enough to get some flowers. What about, Fred?"

Damn! She'd forgotten about Fred. She knew Theresa would have bought him some flowers, had she not joined the Army, and was now stationed in South Carolina for basic combat training.

"I'll get him some," Shonda promised.

Leaving the jail, Shonda withdrew money from the nearest ATM teller, bought two sets of flowers, then headed for her house on Joseph Court, that she was able to buy with some of the money she'd made working for James at Kingz BMWs before it was burned down. She heard that it was back up and running under a new name.

"Not now, Mario!" she said to herself as she pulled into her driveway to see Mario sitting on the steps of her porch.

To her, what they had was a sex thing, although he claimed he was so in love with her. He was not all that in the face, but he was 6'1", brown-skinned and muscular, just the way she liked her men. Plus, he held nothing back in the bedroom, but her patience was wearing thin with him being unemployed. He would lay-up in her house, eat her food, and spend her money, but couldn't conduce to her utilities, or her welfare. The sex was good, but it wasn't enough. He swore he loved her, and that was definitely not enough, but she respected his feelings, which is why she left the flowers on the back seat when she dismounted.

"You look lost," she asserted as she approached.

"I'm always lost without you," he replied, standing.

"I don't wanna hear that Romeo and Juliet shit!" she said, dodging the kiss he tried to greet her with as she brushed past him to the front door. "Have you found a job yet?"

"Not yet, baby," he admitted, kissing her on the back of her neck, and gripping her butt as she unlocked the door, "but I'm trying."

"Apparently, you ain't trying hard enough." She entered the house, punching in her code on the alarm pad.

"I am," Mario insisted. "These White folks ain't trying to hire a nigga."

"Any excuse is better than none, huh?"

She headed for the bedroom and began undressing, disregarding Mario, who'd showed up seconds later and leaned against the threshold of the door.

"I'ma get my shit together," Mario promised.

Shonda didn't care to respond. Now, in her panties and bra, she laid her uniform pants and shirt on the back of a chair and was ready to take her shower, but Mario had the door blocked.

"Move, Mario!" she demanded.

Mario didn't budge. He was lustfully eyeing her, but she already knew that his pussy-hungry ass was going to want some, once he'd caught a glimpse of her half-naked body.

"Boy move!" she tried again, stepping closer, standing an inch shorter than him. "You ain't finna get no pussy. I gotta shower, and—"

Mario made his move, wrapping his arms around her waist and planting his mouth on hers, stifling her words.

"Uh-uh, Mario!"

She broke the kiss, but Mario was relentless, moving his mouth down to her neck which was her hot spot.

"Mario, please!" Her voice was just above a whisper as she looked towards the ceiling with half-squinted pupils.

One part of her wanted to resist, but the other part was begging to be pleased. After two nights of masturbating herself to sleep, her will to resist, slowly declined as he lowered her onto the bed and pulled her panties off. Being that he wasn't adept with the handling of a woman's bra, she took the initiative. That's when Mario, hungrily tackled her breasts with his mouth, licking and sucking her fully erect nipples. She moaned, and almost grabbed his head, before remembering he was a real cry baby about messing up his waves. Instead, she let her arms fall to her sides and gripped the bedspread.

Mario stopped, got undressed, and was back on top of her, hungrier than before. He sucked her nipples so hard, they started to hurt. She wanted to protest but feeling his rock-hard dick pressed against her inner thigh, gave her the courage to hold out. Then, he moved down to her navel, probing it with his tongue as he inserted two fingers into her vagina. She loved his pattern of foreplay, but this was taking entirely too long. Therefore, she gingerly placed a hand atop his head, and pushed him downward, half-expecting him go grouch about his hair, but he didn't. He obediently and greedily attacked her clitoris like a ravenous animal, almost causing her to explode in his face.

"Ooh, baby, I'm about to come!" she shrieked.

Mario didn't stop, instead, he inserted his two fingers for assistance to make sure she did just that. She didn't have any resistance left in her so when she reached her peak, all she could do was let it flow, and allow him to taste her honey. Then, not giving her a chance to exhale, Mario quickly mounted her, lifted her leg, and rammed every inch of his manhood inside of her.

"Ooh, shit!" she exclaimed, gripping his waist, forcing him to thrust harder and deeper.

Mario would usually put her in different positions, but he maintained this position until they both exploded. Then, instead of laying on top of her and drowning her in kisses like he would always do, he got up and went into the adjacent bathroom to wash up, leaving her stunned and breathless, but it was all good because she'd gotten some. They'd been together off and on for five months, and she still hadn't figured out why he wouldn't let her perform oral sex on him. She pondered that on her way to the main bathroom to take her shower.

After showering and donning one of her jean suits, Shonda grabbed her car keys and entered the living room, where Mario was fully dressed, sitting on the sofa with his foot up on the coffee table.

"Boy get your damn foot off my table!" she demanded, "and I hope your greedy ass washed every dish you messed up!"

"Where you, going?" he asked.

"I gotta meet up with, Sheila and Ebony. Why?"

"I need a ride back to the trap."

"You ain't gon' spend the night?"

"I'll be back later."

She knew it was a lie, but instead of going there with him, she returned to her bedroom for her purse, and they exited the house.

"When are you gonna give me a key to the house?" Mario asked once they were inside the car.

"When you start paying bills," she answered, pulling out of the driveway.

"So, our relationship is based on money?"

"Trust me—" she started. "If our relationship was based on money, we wouldn't have a relationship. I'm not asking you to take care of me. I take care of myself, but if you're my man, you should be able to help me out from time to time. Not just physically, but mentally and financially, also."

"I'm working on the finance part," he asserted.

"How many times have I heard that?" she asked. "How long do you—"

"Who bought you some flowers?" he cut her off.

"Nobody." She had almost forgotten about the flowers.

"Well, who gave you some flowers?"

"Nobody."

"So, how'd you get flowers in your back seat?"

"I put 'em there."

Mario was now staring at her, but she kept her eyes on the road. She was really hoping he's let it go because she'd never told him about her relationship with James and didn't intend to.

"So, you ain't gon' tell me the truth?" he pushed.

She ignored him.

"No response, huh?" he persisted. "If I throw 'em out the window, would I get a response then?"

"Mario, if you touch those flowers," she stated slowly, "the only response you'll get is me on your ass! Now, try me if you think I'm playing!"

Apparently, he believed her, because he was quiet for the remainder of the ride. She kind of felt bad for talking to him like that, but, right now she was not in the mood for his unstable behavior.

"I'm not going all the way in," she said as she entered East Lake Meadows, making a U-turn at the entrance.

"How long will you be out?" Mario asked.

"Not too long. I do have to work in the morning."

Mario looked like he was in deep thought.

"What's wrong?" she inquired.

"I gotta re-up," he told her, "but I need about two hundred more dollars."

"And you're asking me for two hundred dollars?" she asked nonchalantly to his request.

"If you don't mind, I'll pay you back."

"Mario, how many times have you borrowed money and paid me back?" she asked. "And how do you sell all this dope, and ain't never got no money?"

"I'm trying to go half on a brick with another kat," he explained. "That's the only way I'll be able to make some real money and help you out on the bills."

Shonda just looked at him. She knew he was gaming her as always. Every time she vowed to not lend him any more money, she would always go back on her word. So, once again, she went back on her word and gave him the money. She just looked at it as if she paid for sex, as always.

It was well after five when Shonda made it to Gwinnett County and pulled into the plaza where Ebony's beauty salon Glamour Girlz was located. She parked and as she was getting out, saw Ebony and Sheila coming her way.

"You ready?" Ebony asked.

"You're not gonna close up?" Shonda asked, seeing that there were still people inside the salon.

"Khandi's got it," Ebony answered. "She got one more head to do anyway."

Shonda asked, "Y'all got flowers?"

"Yeah," they answered in unison.

"Well, I guess we're ready."

They all climbed into their cars and drove out to the cemetery on Martin Luther King Drive. Dismounting and carrying flowers, they branched off, being that The Kingz especially Ray and James were not buried near each other.

Being that she'd bought flowers for Fred also, Shonda journeyed to his grave first which took some time to find. After a moment of silence, and bidding him to rest in peace, she laid the flowers on his grave, then headed for James' grave. She didn't know what to say, so she just stood there in silence, thinking about the times they had together, and everything she learned from him. If it wasn't for James, she would probably still be working fast foods, and sharing an apartment with Sheila, with no car. So, she was more than grateful to be standing at this grave with some flowers that were in no way sufficient to proclaim her gratitude.

"I miss you, Jay!" she finally spoke. "No matter what happens in my life, or how old I get. I'll never forget you, or the things you've taught me."

CHAPTER 2

After leaving the cemetery, Ebony retreated to her house in Gwinnett County, that she shared with her fiancé, Charles. They met in
January, he proposed to her in April bought her the salon in May,
and moved her in, the following month. That's when she was finally able to meet his six-year-old daughter, Robyn whose mother
he admits to still be on good terms with. Ebony didn't suspect him
of sleeping with her or any other woman because he's a God-fear-
ing, and church-going man.

Ebony arrived home and parked her white Infiniti, a birthday
present from Charles in the driveway beside Charles' black, four-
door Jaguar. When she entered the house, she was immediately hit
by the aroma of various seasons of cooked food. This made her
stomach growl, reminding her that she had not eaten since breakfast,
which was a couple of Power Bars, and a cup of coffee. She'd
planned on eating a heavy lunch, but after getting the call from
Shonda, reminding her of what today was, she'd forgotten all about
lunch.

"Hey, baby!" Ebony greeted her fiancé, who was 5'9", dark-
brown skinned, and a bit on the chubby side. He was at the stove,
stirring up something in a pot.

"Hey, sweetheart!" he returned her greeting as she kissed him
on the jaw. "I thought you had gotten lost."

"No," she answered with a sigh. "Sheila and Shonda stopped by
to see me."

Charles had never just come out and said it, but Ebony knew he
didn't agree with her friends. Every time she'd bring them up, he
would appear uninterested and change the subject, but he'd never
said anything offensive about them.

"You got a letter from, Theresa," he now told her.

"Yeah?" This was good news because she had not heard from
her friend in two months, thinking that they'd sent her across the
seas to fight the war.

Ebony found the letter on the dresser in their bedroom, along
with the other mail. She immediately tore open the envelope, sat on

the edge of the bed, and read the letter. Theresa said she was okay, but she was having complications during the exercise drills. She also said she'd heard rumors that she would be discharged for medical reasons.

Ebony didn't know if she should be happy or feel sad for Theresa, who'd joined the Army in search of a better career and opportunities. She placed the letter back inside the envelope, put it in the top drawer with her other mail, then joined Charles at the dining room table, where they dined on beef stew, mashed potatoes, garlic bread, and salad.

"How's your meal?" Charles asked, regarding her with a worried look.

"Huh?" She noticed his look and realized she must have been consuming her food like a starving orphan.

"Are you okay?" he inquired. "You seem hungry."

"I didn't eat lunch," she said apologetically.

"Why not?"

"Loss of appetite."

"Well, I'm glad you've found it," he stated, regarding her with a warm smile. "So, how was your day?"

"The usual," she answered, taking a sip of her lemonade. "The gossip column was in effect. Pam and her boyfriend broke up again. How was yours, did you sell the house?"

He took a sip of lemonade before answering. "The couple backed out, claiming an emergency."

"What was the emergency?"

"I didn't ask," he answered. "Whatever it was, I'm quite sure it was personal, but I have someone else lined up for it."

As always, Ebony and Charles made small conversation as they finished their dinner. Charles was thirty-four years old nine years older than Ebony with a degree in Business, Medicine, and Psychology, but worked as a Realtor. A person could tell by his demeanor, and the way he talked, he wasn't the street type. Ebony was content with that because she was tired of dealing with hood niggas who only limited themselves to the streets and didn't want anything out of life. Charles wasn't much to look at, but he was all that she'd wanted in a man, and he knew how to treat his woman. So, yes, she was more than happy to walk down the aisle with him, even though this would be his second time.

****

"Log me in for a security check," Officer Price told Shonda.

Shonda waited until Price had left the booth to conduct the security round before logging her in. Then, she was back to watching the men in the recreation yard as they worked out with their shirts off. She just wished that Sheila was on post with her, but unfortunately, Lieutenant Mallery had other plans for Sheila, sending her back to eight North-East with Officer Grant.

"What's up, Ms. Watson!"

Shonda looked to her right to see the inmate whose name she'd forgotten who always managed to make his way to the booth, whenever she was alone. He wasn't her type, he was dark-skinned, with more stomach than chest, but she found him entertaining in an uncanny way.

"What'd you want boy?" she asked.

"Boy!" he exclaimed. "You don't know a man when you see one?"

"I guess not," she replied, playfully eyeing him. "You ain't even old enough to buy alcohol."

"I can't tell. Money can buy whatever you want it to buy."

Shonda eyed him, she knew what he was implying, but she wasn't going that route again. This was the same way she'd met Mario when he was locked up.

"Don't make me write you up," Shonda threatened, pretending to put up a barricade.

"Or, you can just write your number down," he said, leaning on the desk.

Shonda found that funny. "You better go somewhere and play, lil boy! Y'all ain't got that long out. You could be on the phone with your family, instead of wasting your time at this desk."

"Where're you from, shawty?"

Playa Ray

"I'm not your, shawty," she protested, "and where I'm from is none of your business. Where are *you* from?"

"I'm from Bankhead, Cedar Avenue."

"So, what're you doing in the Dekalb County Jail?"

He answered, "I caught a trafficking charge, right up the street from this muhfucka."

"It ain't like you had no bricks," she ventured, looking around for Price, who was standing by the TV, conversing with other inmates.

"What you know about some bricks?" he asked, giving her a look of suspicion.

"Don't let this uniform fool you," she told him. "I know more than you think I know."

****

"You watch football?" Grant asked Sheila, who was tending to her crossword puzzle book she'd brought along to keep herself entertained.

"Nope," she answered, not taking her eyes off the book.

"Basketball?"

"Nope."

"Am I disturbing you?"

"Not really."

Truth was, his presence alone was disturbing her, which was why she'd brought the book, figuring Lieutenant Mallery was going to pull this stunt again. She'd done a good job of avoiding eye contact with him, but there was no denying the mixture of his soap and cologne had her senses all scrambled, causing her to cross out words that would never be found in anyone's dictionary. The only time she was able to collect her wits, was during the hiatus of Grant's absence from the desk. Then, she would pleasingly take in the cool air-conditioned air as if she'd been held under water for a long period of time.

"You seem bothered about something," Grant prodded. "I guess that book is helping you to keep your mind off of it, or him."

22

That's when she finally made eye contact. "Excuse me?"

"I mean there's nothing wrong with that," he vouched. "Everybody—"

"Maybe I just like doing puzzles," she cut him off. "Have you thought about that?"

"That was my first thought," he insisted.

"Yeah right."

She diverted her attention from him to survey the dorm when one inmate caught her attention. He was standing at one of the telephones, watching her, with the receiver to his ear, and one hand down the front of his jail-issued uniform pants. She could already tell what he was doing, by the slight movement of his arm.

"I swear!" Grant carried on, "but you just don't seem like the type that would do crossword puzzles, just to be doing them. That's why I went with my second thought, but if you took it as an insult, I apologize!"

"Look at this perverted-ass man!" she spoke through clenched teeth.

At this time, the inmate had pulled his dick out and was slowly stroking it, but when Grant looked in his direction, he quickly shoved his dick back inside his pants and tried to pretend like he wasn't looking in their direction.

"Take your nasty ass to your cell!" Grant hollered to the guy, who was now pretending to be talking to someone on the phone. "So, you're just gonna try and play me like I'm stupid?" Grant tried again, getting everyone's attention, well everyone's except the culprit, who was hell-bent on maintaining his innocent façade.

Furious, Grant lunged from his chair and vigorously approached the man who was now regarding him with apprehension. Sheila watched as Grant grabbed the guy by his shirt and yanked him away from the phone, leaving the receiver clashing against the pillar that the phone was mounted to. The guy was now trying to plead with Grant, who had him jacked up by his shirt, escorting him to his cell, where he locked himself inside with him.

At this time, the other inmates had stopped what they were doing and began voicing their opinions. Sheila stood, not knowing if she should call a ten seventy-eight over the radio, or what, because clearly Grant's antic was sure to excite a riot. It was incontestable that Grant had locked himself in the cell with the inmate to presumably rough him up, but Sheila was tempted to go and check, just in case it was the other way around, but as soon as she thought it, the lock on the cell door clicked, and Grant emerged, slamming the door behind him. His shirt was ruffled and partly untucked. When he reached the booth, Sheila could see small specks of blood on his uniform.

Grant pressed the Talk button on the PA system: "Free-time is now over, lock it down!" After listening to the inmates' grump and complain about having five minutes left, he said, "If I get to your cell and lock the door, and you're not inside that cell, you're gonna wish you were!"

They watched as the inmates reluctantly retreated to their cells. Sheila was shocked, but, at the same time, thrilled by how Grant handled the situation. She didn't intend for him to beat the inmate up, or conclude free-time ahead of time, but witnessing his take-charge attitude, sparked something inside of her.

****

'*Thank God it's Friday*!' Shonda thought to herself as she exited the building, headed for her car.

She and Sheila managed to get the same off-days, which were Saturday and Sunday. After a slew of dreary weekends, Shonda decided those days were over. She didn't have any definite plans, but she was determined to find some entertainment, somewhere. Maybe she would drag Sheila to a club tonight. She already knew Charles was not going to let Ebony anywhere near a club.

Shonda's car was parked two cars away from Sheila's, so after starting it and letting the top down, she perched on the trunk and waited for Sheila, who was to show her the letter from Theresa, who always addressed her letters to them both, thinking they still lived in the same apartment. At that time, Sheila emerged from the building, smiling and giggling like a high school girl. Alongside her was

Grant, who Shonda figured to be the cause of it. He walked her to her car, where they talked for a brief moment, then he headed for his car. Shonda locked eyes with him as he passed. Once their eyes disconnected, hers dropped to his butt as her mind began to undress him.

"You know, stalking is a felony."

Shonda looked to see Sheila standing akimbo, with a white envelope in her hand.

"Girl, please!" Shonda said. "I was thinking something along the line of kidnapping!"

Sheila laughed. "Girl, you're crazy!"

"I see y'all done got acquainted," Shonda accused, with raised eyebrows.

"It ain't even like that," Sheila replied, handing her the envelope.

"I told you he can charm the panties off a mannequin," Shonda stated with a mischievous grin.

"Mannequins don't have brains," Sheila pointed out. "So, he'll need more than charm to get *these* panties off."

"Okay." Shonda was skeptical. "You got plans for tonight?"

****

Sheila could not believe she'd let Shonda con her into going to a club. Now, she was seated at the bar, sipping a club soda, while Shonda was out on the floor, dancing, and having a good time, but as she watched her cousin, her mind was elsewhere. Yea, she was thinking about, Grant.

Each time Grant entered her mind, there was mental pictures of him sexing her in different positions, which got her juices flowing. Then, she would realize her eyes were closed, and her legs were shaking. She tried to parry the thoughts by thinking of other people but failed. Not even thoughts of Ray would avail. This frustrated her because she knew why her body was responding the way it did.

She had not had sex in almost three months, so she was long over-due, and in dire need of a man to pin her down and ram a flagpole inside of her.

"Either you're drunk, tired, or just bored as hell."

Sheila snapped her eyes open and stopped her legs from shak-ing. Now, she was just staring at the dark-skinned, bald-headed guy, who had just spoken to her.

"I'm J.T.," he said, holding his hand out.

"Sheila," she responded shaking his hand, but quickly let it go being that she was so horny the slightest touch from a man could send her into an orgasm.

"You looked like you were falling asleep over here," he acknowledged.

"I was just vibing," she lied.

"I feel that. So, who you here with?"

"My cousin," Sheila answered, wishing the music wasn't so loud, so he wouldn't have to stand so close.

"Shit, I'm here with a couple of homeboys," he told her. "What are y'all trying to get into?"

"I'm just chillin'."

"I'm trying to chill wit 'cha."

Sheila just looked at him. She knew he was talking sex, and how she was feeling right now, she would give up her car keys for a man to lay her on the bar and fuck her until her body went limp, but she knew she couldn't just give in to a total stranger. She'd never done that, which is why she was sexually frustrated now.

"I don't know about that," she managed, taking a sip of her drink, and looking out at Shonda, who was grinding her ass on some guy.

"What, it got a price on it?" he asked. "I mean as fine as you are, I wouldn't be surprised."

"Thank you for the compliment, but I'm not a prostitute."

"I didn't mean it like that," he said, apologetically. "I'm just trying to get with you tonight. If I gotta pay to play, I'm with that. If I gotta lick it before I stick it, I'm with that too—front and back."

Sheila didn't know what happened, but somehow, her cup had slipped out of her hand and crashed to the floor. She half-wished the ice-cold beverage would have landed in her lap and seeped through her jeans because this nigga had just poured gasoline on a fire that was already unquenchable.

"You okay?" J.T. asked.

"I'm fine," she lied, flustered. "Excuse me."

Leaving the bar, she quick-stepped through the crowd on the floor to Shonda, and grabbed her by the arm, pulling her away from the man she was dancing with.

"Girl, what's wrong with your crazy ass!" Shonda asked, laughing.

"I gotta go!" Sheila answered.

Shonda was no longer laughing. "Why, somebody bothering you?"

'*Yeah, my pussy,*' Sheila thought, but said, "No, I'm just tired. Besides, I'm not feeling this atmosphere."

Playa Ray

CHAPTER 3

Sheila managed to pull herself out of bed, a little after 10 am, ate breakfast, showered, and got dressed. She and Shonda had appointments at Ebony's salon, which is why she'd taken her hair down last night, after coming home from the club, where she parted ways with Shonda, who decided to stay a little longer.

It had taken Sheila almost two hours to undo her hair, which, to her was good, because it kept her hands from doing what she really needed them to do. Well, that was until she climbed into bed and started having hot flashes to the point where she couldn't sleep until she was relieved of some of the sexual tension that was build up inside. Masturbation became her nostrum.

"Hey, girl!" Shonda greeted Sheila when she entered the salon. She was seated in Ebony's chair, as Ebony applied extensions.

"Girl, you look like you had a rough night!" Ebony voiced.

"Hello to you, too!" Sheila said, then greeted the other stylists as she took a seat in the waiting area.

"You alright, baby?" Shonda questioned.

"I'm good," Sheila answered, looking past Khandi, to the large vanity mirror to see if she could see what her friends were seeing. "Do I really look like I had a rough night?"

"Or woke up on the wrong side of the bed," said Ebony. "Who done pissed you off?"

"Nobody," she answered, still checking her image in the mirror. "I didn't get much sleep last night."

"Late night booty call!" Pam implied, getting a laugh from everyone in the salon, including Sheila.

On the days Sheila and Shonda were scheduled to get their hair fixed once a month, Ebony would only do their hair, and take the rest of the day off, leaving Khandi to lock up, so she could spend the day with her friends.

After doing their hair, Ebony insisted they ride in her car. They drove to South Dekalb Mall where they purchased a few outfits and shoes. After leaving the mall, they decided to have lunch at Red Lobster.

Y'all know my baby's birthday is in two weeks, right?" Ebony said to her friends, who were both seated across from her.

"Baby!" Shonda exclaimed. "That nigga's damn near old enough to be your, daddy!"

"He is not!" Ebony defended.

"Well, he *looks* old enough," Shonda persisted. "In two weeks, he'll be what—fifty?" Ebony scowled at Shonda and Sheila laughed. "Plus, he acts like he's your dad," Shonda continued. "He tells you who to hang around, what time to be in the house, and how to dress. Hell, you gotta play hooky from work to hang out with people you've known your whole life. We always swore to never let a man come between us. It seems like somebody's slipping."

Ebony realized Shonda was serious, and her accusation was undoubtedly true. Ever since she'd been with Charles, she hardly had time to spend with her friends, with running a business from Monday through Saturday, and spending Sunday's with Charles, which consisted of church services, visiting, or having family members over for dinner, and come to think about it, not once had she invited her friends over for Sunday dinner.

"You're right," Ebony conceded. "I let my new life take me away from my friends, and I apologize. How can I make it up to y'all?"

"You can wash my car," Shonda offered.

"Hell, you can just buy me a new one," Sheila added.

"How 'bout I invite y'all over to my house tomorrow, for Sunday dinner?" Ebony offered.

****

"Daddy, I'm hungry!" Robyn whined from the back seat.

It was after twelve, and Ebony, Charles, and Robyn had just left church and were en route to visit Ebony's mother, who still resided in Stone Mountain, Georgia. Then, they were to return home, where they were going to start preparing dinner for their guests, which consisted of Charles' mother, brother, and his brother's girlfriend.

Plus, Shonda and Sheila, their surprise guests. Well, they were going to be a surprise to Charles, because Ebony was not going to tell him they were coming.

"What do you want to eat, sweetheart?" Charles asked his daughter.

"I want a Happy Meal!" she answered, gleefully.

Charles looked over at Ebony, who nodded and headed for the nearest McDonald's, where they dined in. Then, leaving there, they journeyed out to Stone Mountain.

"Come on in y'all!" Ebony's mother said, letting them in. "Y'all look good!"

"Thank you, Ms. Davis!" replied Charles.

"Mama, you got it smelling good in here!" Ebony commented.

"That's your greedy sister in there eating up my bacon," Ms. Davis said.

"Erica's in there?" Ebony was shocked because it had been nine months since she'd seen her older sister, who'd migrated to Chicago to be with a man who'd jilted her, two months later, leaving her out on the streets to fend for herself.

"Child, I don't know who that is in there!" her mother expressed with a worried look on her face.

"Y'all have a seat," Ebony told Charles and Robyn. "I'll be right back."

As soon as Ebony entered the kitchen, she stopped dead in her tracks. She could clearly see what her mother was saying. This was definitely not the Erica they remembered. Her short hair was disheveled, and her dingy, loose-fitted jeans indicated she'd lost a great deal of weight. She no longer possessed the shape most of the women in their family were known for.

She watched as Erica, who had her back to her, turn off the stove and piled bacon between two slices of toasted bread that were on a saucer on the counter. Then, as if not seeing Ebony standing there, Erica took a seat at the table and attacked her sandwich like she had not eaten in days. This churned Ebony's heart because she couldn't even imagine half of the things her sister had been through. She poured Erica a glass of orange juice before taking a seat across from her, which gave her a closer look at Erica's face that was sunken in and revealed her bone structure.

"I know, I look bad," Erica admitted as if reading her thoughts, "and no, I'm not on drugs."

"Alcohol?" Ebony ventured, noticing she sounded as if she was tired.

"Occasionally," she answered, taking a sip of her juice.

"When did you get back?"

"Today, Mama said you're doing good."

"I'm doing better than I was."

"Your man bought you a beauty salon," Erica acknowledged. "You're doing damn good!"

"Where are you staying?" Ebony asked, changing the subject.

"Here, until mama kicks me out," she answered. "Or, until I find a man with some money."

"You haven't learned yet, Erica."

"All men are not the same, Ebony."

"You won't know until they drag you all the way to Chicago and leave you stranded," Ebony asserted, locking eyes with her sister.

"Don't speak on things you don't know about," Erica countered finishing up her sandwich and juice.

"You called mama and told her he kicked you out," Ebony pointed out. "What more do I need to know?"

"Did you ever stop to think that I may have been the reason for what happened?"

"Nope." Ebony was not willing to diminish the hatred she had for the man who'd dogged her sister. Someone she'd looked up to her whole life.

"Well, *I am* the reason," Erica admitted, "and I don't blame him for being a man."

This had Ebony thinking. She was trying to figure out what could Erica have possibly done to make him kick her out. It had to be something real serious, that he couldn't will himself to forgive her for.

"Don't rack your brains, lil sis," Erica said. "What's done, is done."

"Why didn't you just come home when he kicked you out?"

"I didn't have any money."

"So, you were living in the streets?"

"I was staying at a shelter until I started dancing at a club," Erica answered. "Then I shacked up with one of the other dancers. When the manager realized I was pregnant, he fired me saying it wouldn't look right for a pregnant woman to be dancing at a strip club."

"You were pregnant!" Ebony could not believe this. "Did that nigga know you were pregnant when he kicked you out?"

"Yeah, he knew," answered Erica. "I spent the rest of my money on an abortion, and a bus ticket."

"So, this nigga kicked you out, knowing you were pregnant?" Ebony rephrased her question.

"It wasn't his baby, Ebony."

****

Ebony thought about her sister, during the drive home, and while she and Charles prepared dinner, with the supervision of Robyn. Periodically, Charles would ask, if she was okay. She had never lied to Charles, but there were things about her personal life she did not disclose to him. This revelation of her sister was just another chapter in her book.

"I'm okay," she answered him for the fourth time as the door-bell rang.

"Daddy, is that grandmama?" Robyn asked.

"I don't know," Charles answered, wiping his hands on his apron. "Let's go and see!"

Once again, Ebony was left to her thoughts, when they'd left the kitchen to answer the door. She knew it wasn't her friends, because they weren't due for another half-hour, or so, but she still kept her ears perked up, while she checked on the meatloaf. She was a bit relieved when she heard Robyn cheerfully greet her grandmother and Uncle Eugene. She'd also heard the voice of Michelle, Eugene's girlfriend, who never had much to say to Ebony. Perhaps she had noticed that Eugene had wandering eyes.

"Hello, my future daughter-in-law!" Charles' mother entered the kitchen, all smiles.

"Hey, Ms. Bernice!" Ebony dried her hands on a towel, before embracing her.

"How are you?" Ms. Bernice asked.

"I'm hanging in there."

"Praise the Lord!" Bernice replied. "You need any help in here?"

"No ma'am, we're almost done. If you give me a minute, I'll bring y'all some drinks and appetizers."

It took her and Charles almost ten minutes to prepare a tray of crackers and cheese and glasses of grape juice. Ebony greeted Eugene and Michelle as she placed the tray on the coffee table. She didn't have to look at Eugene, to know that he was undressing her with his eyes, as always. She wanted to bring it to Charles' attention but knew that it would be futile, being that Charles was overly fond of his baby brother. But Ebony saw something in Eugene that Charles didn't, or couldn't see— envy!

"So, Eugene, how's the new job treating you?" Charles asked, once he and Ebony had taken their seats on the love-seat, across from their guests and Robyn, who was sitting on the floor beside the coffee table.

"It's paying the bills," Eugene answered. "Puts food on the table."

"Hey, if you don't work, you don't eat," Charles told him.

"Easy for you to say."

"How's that?"

"You got it made," Eugene pointed out, casting a glance at Ebony. "Everybody's not as lucky as you."

As if it was her cue, Ebony excused herself and headed for the kitchen to check on the meatloaf and cornbread. She was thinking Charles had to have seen the way Eugene looked at her. Michelle wasn't as good-looking as Ebony, but she wasn't a bad-looking woman. It's typical for a woman to call a man like Eugene a dog, but Ebony was sticking to her guns on this one. Eugene envied Charles! After taking the bread out of the oven, Ebony made two trips out to the garage for two more dining chairs. Then, she returned to the living room.

"Still waiting on the meatloaf," Ebony said as she re-took her seat.

The conversation resumed for another ten minutes before Ebony excused herself to check on the meatloaf again. While she was taking it out of the oven, she heard the doorbell and immediately knew who it was. Therefore, she placed the dish on the stove and hurried out of the kitchen.

"I got it!" she yelled out as she approached the door.

She opened the door to Shonda and Sheila, who to her surprise had taken the initiative to dress appropriately for the occasion.

"Girl, y'all look fabulous!" Ebony commented. "Come on in!"

They entered the living room, where Ebony made proper introductions disregarding the disapproving look Charles was giving her and announced that dinner was ready. Ms. Bernice offered to help Ebony bring the dishes to the table. As they did, Ebony did a good job of avoiding eye contact with Charles. Ms. Bernice said grace, and everyone dug in.

"So, Sheila and Shonda, what do you ladies do for a living?" Ms. Bernice asked.

"We're detention officers," Sheila answered.

"At a jail?" Ms. Bernice seemed surprised.

"At the Dekalb County Jail."

"I don't think a woman should work in places like jails and prisons," Ms. Bernice asserted with a disgusted look on her face.

Shonda took offense. "Why not?"

"I just don't feel a lady should work in places like that, around dangerous criminals," she admitted.

"We don't judge them," replied Shonda, "and everybody that's locked up, are not bad people. They just made the wrong choices."

Ms. Bernice looked like she was considering what Shonda said. "You know, I've never looked at it that way. The Bible says, *Thou shalt not judge, and Judge not, that ye not be judged.* Do you ladies attend church?"

Sheila and Shonda exchanged glances.

"I'll take that as a no," said Ms. Bernice, smiling. "We attend a small church, but—"

"Mama, you can't just go around forcing religion on people," Charles intervened.

I'm not forcing religion on them, Charles," she countered. "I'm just inviting them to attend—"

"They may have other things to do," he cut her off again.

"My friends would love to attend, Ms. Bernice," Ebony spoke up, not liking how this conversation was going. "They'll be there, next Sunday."

Ebony knew she was getting skeptical looks from Charles, Sheila, and Shonda, but ignored them as she tended to her meal. The conversation didn't resume for the next five minutes until Eugene asked Charles about renting a house from him.

When dinner was over, and everyone was ready to leave, Ebony walked her friends out to their cars that were parked at the curb.

"Ebony, how the hell you gon' volunteer us to go to church, without our permissions?" Shonda asked once they made it to the vehicles.

"We'll talk about that later," Ebony answered. "Erica got back in town today."

"For real?" asked Sheila.

"Yeah," Ebony answered, then told them everything Erica had told her.

"Sounds like she had a rough time," Shonda commented.

"She done lost a lot of weight too," Ebony added.

"Drugs?"

"She denied it, but she admitted to drinking."

At that time, Ms. Bernice, Eugene, and Michelle exited the house, followed by Charles. They all said their farewells to the girls, before climbing into an old-model Cadillac, driven by Eugene, and rode off. Charles retreated inside.

"What you and Eugene got going on?" Shonda asked with raised eyebrows. "I saw how he was watching you."

"Yeah, I saw that, too," said Sheila.

"Charles is the only person in the world who can't see it," Ebony said. "He's always watching me."

"Why don't you tell, Charles?" Sheila wanted to know.

"It wouldn't do any good."

After hugging and bidding her friends good night, she headed back inside the house, where Charles was in Robyn's room, getting her ready to go. Ebony proceeded on to their bedroom to prepare for her shower.

"You didn't tell me your friends were coming over," Charles asserted when he entered the room, buttoning up his coat.

"And you didn't tell me they were not welcome here," she said, accusingly, staring at him through the dresser's mirror.

"Bye, Ms. Ebony!"

Ebony diverted her attention to Robyn who was now standing in the doorway with her bookbag on her back.

"Can I have a hug before you go?" Ebony asked.

"Yes."

"Be a good girl." Ebony embraced and kissed her on the cheek.

"We'll talk when I get back," Charles told Ebony, escorting Robyn out of the room.

"That's what *you* think," Ebony mumbled to herself.

She was going to shower and climb into bed. As far as she was concerned, a conversation about her friends was irrelevant, because if they were not welcome here, neither was she.

Playa Ray

CHAPTER 4

"You must've left your crossword book in the car?" Grant asked Sheila when he returned to the desk from doing a security check.

"I was done with that one," she answered. "I'll have to buy another one, today."

It was already after ten, and the day had been running smooth. Sheila and Grant had made casual conversation, although Grant had done all the talking, telling her about the drama he was going through with his son's mother. The things he'd told her, made her feel compassionate towards him. Being that he – from what he'd claimed – was doing everything he could for his son, the mother was still threatening him with child support.

"Is that what you do at home?" he now asked.

"What?"

"Crossword puzzles," he answered. "I mean, not to make it seem like you're just sitting at home, bored, doing crossword puzzles, but—"

"Yes, I sit at home, bored, doing crossword puzzles," she admitted, cutting him off.

"I didn't mean it like that."

"It's the truth," she confirmed.

"Can't be."

"Why not?"

"Because that's a bad sign."

"A bad sign of what?"

Grant sighed, before answering, "If you have a man at home, and have to resort to a puzzle book for entertainment, then, something's not right."

"But what if I don't have a man at home?" she asked, looking into his light-brown eyes.

"Well, we both know that's not true," he said, sounding uncertain.

She just stared at him. As she did, she saw his expression go from disbelieving, to inquisitive.

"I can't go for that one, Griffin," he asserted. "That's unthinkable, ain't no way in hell!"

Sheila laughed. "You act like you ain't never met a single woman before."

"I've met plenty of single women," he replied. "I've also met plenty of women who *claimed* to be single but had multiple sex partners."

"It sounds like you get around, Mr. Grant," she expressed with raised eyebrows.

"It's not even like that," he contended.

"Oh?"

Before he could reply, the buzzer on the panel sounded. Simultaneously, they looked at the panel, then to the sally port, where the panel had indicated the call was coming from. Sheila didn't know about Grant, but Lieutenant Mallery was the last person she'd expected to be standing there.

"You gon' buzz her in?" Grant asked.

Sheila furrowed her eyebrow at him.

"Well, excuse me!" he said, smiling, buzzing Mallery in.

"Kill on the floor!" one of the inmates yelled out when Mallery entered the dorm, which made Sheila smile to herself.

"Your mama!" Mallery retorted. "I wish one of y'all would pull your lil' nasty dick out on me! I'ma break it off and stick it up ya ass!"

Her comment won laughter from the inmates, but neither one of them defied to reply to it.

"Hey, Andrew!" Mallery greeted Grant as she approached and stood in front of the booth.

"What up, Lieutenant?" Grant returned her greeting, handing her the logbook.

"I can't call it," she answered, pulling out a pen to sign the book. "Um, Officer Griffin, according to the log-book, it's time for a security check."

"Officer Grant just did a security check," Sheila said as calm as she could.

"Officer Griffin," Mallery asserted slowly, with much authority, "according to the logbook, it's time for a security check."

Sheila already knew where this was going. The hatred Mallery has for her was evident, and she was trying her best to push Sheila into a conniption fit, so she could hit her with insubordination and cause her, her job.

Well, at this moment, Sheila was in no position to lose her job. Therefore, she obediently got up and headed for the recreation yard, where she was going to begin. The inmates on the top tier were out on their free time, so she started on the bottom range. As she moved along, pretending to look in on the inmates, she glanced over at the booth and saw that Mallery had taken a seat, and was visibly flirting with Grant, but Sheila disregarded the act knowing she was only doing this to make her jealous.

Well, although she would never admit it, it was working. Making it to the guy's cell, who Grant had roughed up last week, Sheila couldn't help but look in to see that he and his cellmate were sitting on the bottom bunk, playing cards. They didn't see her. She proceeded on, clearing the bottom range, then ascended the stairs to the top range. By the time she was halfway across, she heard the sally port door slam and saw that Mallery was gone.

"Seems like somebody has a crush on you, Andrew," Sheila stated, when she returned to the desk.

"Do I detect jealousy?" he asked with raised eyebrows.

"Please!" Sheila exclaimed. "Stevie Wonder can see that I look way better than that tramp!"

"And I agree. That's why I can't believe you're single."

"Well, I am," she confirmed, "and, no, I don't have multiple sex partners. That's unladylike."

"Well, since we're both single—" he started, "—can I take you out sometime?"

****

When Shonda pulled into her driveway, she was half-expecting to see Mario sitting on the steps of her porch, but he wasn't. Being that she was in the mood for some company, she grabbed her cell phone and dialed Mario's cell number, only to get his voicemail. She dialed it once more, getting the same results.

Now, she was worried about Mario, because she had not spoken with him since Thursday when she'd dropped him off in East Lake Meadows. This made her wonder if she should drive out to East Lakes, and drag him back to her place, since the weatherman claimed temperatures would be in the low thirties tonight, with a ninety percent chance of rain, and she would need a warm body to snuggle with.

"Fuck it!" she said to herself, putting the car in reverse, and backing out of the driveway.

In lieu of heading straight for East Lake, she stopped at a gas station to grab a box of condoms, being that she was out of birth control pills. She liked Mario, but not enough to have a child by him. She'd promised herself, once she got herself situated, she was going to settle down and have kids, but, right now that promise seemed too far-fetched.

Now, Shonda pulled into the entrance of East Lake Meadows at a slow pace, looking from right to left, hoping to catch Mario out and about, instead of having to pull up to his trap spot. Well, she didn't see him, so she drove on around to where Mario and his other trap buddies were always posted.

As she pulled up, she scanned the small crowd of drug dealers and saw Mario wasn't among them, but the group of men was now looking at her, which was a good enough reason for her not to get out and go to the apartment Mario was always at. Therefore, she blew the horn, hoping he would, at least, peer out the window and see her, but the curtains didn't even move.

She tried again and noticed that other people were now peering out of their windows. Now, she was ready to go. It was bad enough she didn't like coming out to East Lake one of the roughest projects in Decatur, but before pulling off, she decided to try Mario's cell phone again. While she was in the midst of dialing, someone tapped on the driver's window, startling her, almost causing her to drop her phone.

She looked up to see some guy in a large, orange overcoat and matching skull cap. He didn't have a gun in his hand, so Shonda assumed she wasn't about to be jacked for her Mustang that – by the way – was adorned with chrome wheels.

"What?" Shonda asked, annoyed that he was just staring at her.

"Roll the window down," he said.

"For what? I ain't trying to buy nothing."

"I know," he said, calmly. "You're looking for, Mario?"

Shonda took his demeanor, and the mentioning of Mario's name into consideration, and cracked the window a bit. "What, he told you to tell me he ain't out here?" she asked, closing her phone.

"If it was like that," the guy started, "he wouldn't send me out here to do it."

"Why not?"

"Because I feel like that's some bitch-ass shit!"

"What?"

"For a man to send another man to lie for him because he's not man enough to face his woman."

"So, where is he?" she asked, feeling more comfortable with the guy, who seemed to have his morals in order.

"Ain't nobody seen dude, since Friday," he answered. "He got caught up in a deal that went bad, but he's the reason why it went bad." He paused like he was waiting for her to ask what happened. When she didn't, he went on. "Now, he owes some people, and it's not money they want. You're a nice-looking female, and it wouldn't be right for you to get knocked off for his stupidity. So, what you need to do is leave, and don't come back out here. If they can't get him, they'll get you, trust me!"

****

Ebony locked up her salon and, instead of driving straight home, headed for her mother's house. She'd managed to dodge Charles, and the conversation he wanted to have with her about not mentioning her friend's arrival at Sunday dinner, but she knew once she got home, she was going to have to face the music. *So, why not prolong it?*

"Where is she?" Ebony asked when her mother opened the door for her.

"In the kitchen trying to get back what she lost," her mother answered, laughing.

Ebony entered the kitchen and just like her mother stated, Erica was sitting at the table with a plate full of food that looked like leftovers from Sunday dinner, and a large cup of Kool-Aid.

"Hey, big sistah!" Ebony greeted, placing her pocketbook on the table, and pouring herself a glass of Kool-Aid before taking a seat across from Erica.

"You smell like hair products," Erica asserted, wrinkling up her nose.

"I just got off from work," she said, "and speaking of hair, you need to stop by my salon, like yesterday!"

"I have to come all the way to your salon to get my hair fixed?"

"No," Ebony answered. "But I do want you to see my shop and meet the girls. They're cool!"

"I'ma get on y'all about my Kool-Aid!" their mother asserted, upon entering the kitchen, "and, Ebony, I'ma give you my grocery list before you leave."

"Mama, you know I got you if you need money," said Ebony.

"I don't need no money," she answered, "but Erica needs a job. You ain't got nothing for her to do at the shop since she acts like won't nobody else hire her?"

"Not really," Ebony regarded her sister. "Unless you wanna wash hair and do other miscellaneous stuff."

"Like what?" Erica asked, looking as if she knew Ebony was about to say something she was not going to agree with.

"You can't do hair," Ebony pointed out. "So, you can assist me and the girls with our customers, stations and run errands."

"Girl, get for real!" Erica voiced. "I might as well get a job at Burger King or be a janitor at a school."

"Well, that's all I have, Erica."

"Erica, you can't be picky!" their mother intervened. "You gotta start somewhere! It's better than sitting around all day feeling sorry for yourself!"

While their mother was talking, Ebony fished her ringing cell phone from her pocketbook and answered it, seeing it was the house number.

"Are you working late?" Charles asked from the other end.

"No, I'm at my mom's house."

"How long do you plan on being out?"

She almost asked him if he'd given her a curfew but remembered the presence of her mother and sister. She didn't want them to think there were problems between her and Charles although they seemed imminent. "I don't know," she answered his question. "I'll see you when I get home." She ended the call and looked over at her sister. "You can start tomorrow if you want to."

"You ain't even told me how much I'll be getting paid to be your personal flunky," replied Erica.

"We'll discuss that when you show up," Ebony told her. "Mama, would you let her borrow the car?"

"As long as she's working."

Ebony stayed for another twenty minutes, then made her exit. As she drove, she tried to imagine how tonight's conversation was going to go with Charles, and what she was going to say in her friends' defense.

Charles was a good man, and she loved him, but tonight, he was going to accept the fact that her friends were her friends. They were here, way before he'd come into her life, and she was not going to let him destroy their friendship. Shall he feel opposed to that, he could have his engagement ring back tonight! *Along with the car and salon!*

Ebony entered the house expecting Charles to be waiting by the front door, he wasn't. She activated the alarm and headed for the bedroom, knowing for sure he was there, waiting like a father, who was about to catch his child sneaking back into the house after sneaking out. She was wrong again.

As she placed her pocketbook on the dresser, she heard the ding from the microwave, indicating that Charles was, indeed, in the kitchen. Hanging up her coat, she entered the kitchen, where Charles had placed her plate of last night's left-overs, and a cup of juice, on the table. He gestured for her to sit down and leaned his back against the counter with his arms folded over his chest. Ebony took a seat, said a brief grace, then started on her dinner as she awaited Charles' presentation.

"How was your day?" he asked, after watching her consume half of her meal.

She took a sip of her juice to wash her food down before answering. "It was okay, nothing spectacular. How was yours?"

"The same. Finally sold the house in Camden."

Ebony nodded her congratulations and continued eating, feeling this was the moment Charles would speak his mind, but he was silent. Perhaps he hadn't thought of how he was going to approach the subject. Being that Ebony was exhausted and in need of a shower, she finished her dinner and decided she would get the ball rolling.

"What did you wanna talk to me about?" she asked.

He lingered a few seconds, then sat down opposite of her. "I really don't know where or how to start," he admitted. "I can't say you lied, but you invited your friends over without my permission, or even—"

"Your permission!" she cut him off. "If my friends are not welcomed here, you should've told me that before I moved in."

"I didn't say they were not welcomed here," Charles replied.

"But you're saying I was wrong for not telling you they were coming?"

"Basically."

Ebony was ready to get this over with. "Charles, what do you have against my friends?"

"What makes you think that I have something against your friends?"

"Because you always seem to catch an attitude whenever I talk about them," she pointed out. "They may not be Christians, or go to

46

church, but they're my friends, and even they know the Bible teaches against envy and hate."

"I don't hate your friends, Ebony," he professed.

"Well, what is it, Charles? Enlighten me."

Charles looked down at his hands as he fidgeted his fingers, obviously nervous. "I, um," he hesitated. "I believe they'll be our downfall."

"What!" Ebony was beyond shocked. She could not believe he'd actually said that bullshit. "Are you serious?"

"I know how female friends are, Ebony," he asserted. "They be all in your business, feeding you false information, and giving you ill advice that'll have you making false accusations towards your man. That's how most relationships end."

"I agree," Ebony replied. "But these friends you just described, are not my friends." She stood. "And for your information, I don't talk to them, or my co-workers, about what goes on in our household. Now if you don't mind, I would like to take a shower and watch some TV."

Not waiting for a response, she placed her plate and cup in the sink and stormed out of the kitchen.

****

"How did you get caught up with something like that?" Sheila asked Grant over the phone, after listening to another episode about his son's mother.

Sheila knew she was well-overdue, and in need of a companion even if it was just a sex thing so when Grant asked if he could take her out sometime, she was more than happy to give him her number, although she dared to show it, giving him a simple maybe.

"She tricked me," he now answered her question.

"Tricked you?" Sheila giggled, "and how did she manage to do that?"

"She played the good girl role when I met her," he said. "Then, when she got pregnant, all hell broke loose, but it was too late."

"Maybe you just *assumed* she was a good girl," Sheila stated. "You were probably so caught up in her looks, you didn't pay any attention to her demeanor."

"So, you're saying I tricked myself?"

"It's possible, it happens every day."

"That's true," Grant admitted. "So, am I tricking myself now?"

"If I told you, it wouldn't be much of a trick, would it?" she joked, now looking at her cell phone that beeped, indicating someone was calling on the other line. Shonda's number was showing on the screen. "Hold on a minute, Andrew." She clicked over to the other line. "Girl, I'm finna cuss you out!"

"What happened?" Shonda asked.

"I was in the middle of a *good* conversation!" Sheila answered, emphasizing good.

"With who?" Shonda demanded.

"Must you be so nosey?" Sheila teased, not yet ready to tell her about Grant.

"Girl, we need to talk!" Shonda sounded serious. "I really need somebody to talk to, right now. If you can't—"

"Hold on!" Sheila cut her off, switching lines. "Andrew?"

"I'm here."

"That's my cousin," she explained. "She needs to talk to me about something important. I'm sorry!"

"It's okay, just call me whenever you get a chance."

"I will," Sheila switched back over. "Shonda?"

"I'm here."

"Girl, this better be a matter of life and death!"

"As far as I'm concerned, it is!"

CHAPTER 5

Sheila had planned on calling Grant back last night after getting off the phone with Shonda, but Shonda had talked her head off for hours about Mario and what he could have possibly gotten himself into. From what Shonda explained, Mario had pissed off the wrong people and was pretty much a dead man walking.

"What 'cha thinking about?" Grant asked, bringing Sheila out of her reverie.

"Nothing," she lied. "I can't believe it's still raining."

"Yeah, we got a good one, this time," he replied. "You ever been to Dave and Buster's?"

"No," Sheila answered, "but I've always wanted to go. I just haven't found the time."

"How about Friday?" Grant asked. "Then, we can hit the comedy club."

"Are you asking me out on a date?"

Before he could answer, the buzzer sounded on the panel, but Sheila didn't have to regard the panel, because she was already looking at the sally port full of supervisors. Grant immediately buzzed them in. The entourage that consisted of a Captain, two Lieutenants, and two Sergeants, marched up to the desk, looking as if they were about to arrest someone. Lieutenant Mallery grabbed the logbook.

"Officer Griffin conduct a security check!" she instructed.

Sheila didn't know what was going on, but she knew if Mallery wanted to get her fired for insubordination, this would be the best time to do it and the right people to do it in front of. Sheila was nobody's fool, she dutifully stood and left the booth, not making eye contact with either of them. Being that the top range was out on free time, she started upstairs at a slow pace but kept a wary eye on the activity at the booth.

Seconds later, the Captain, both Sergeants, and one of the Lieutenants walked away from the booth, headed for the cells on the bottom range. Mallery who stayed at the booth was going over some papers with Grant.

As Sheila descended the stairs, the other supervisors were walking the inmate that Grant had the physical altercation with, to the sally port with his property. They waited until Mallery had rejoined them before leaving.

"What was that all about?" Sheila asked once she'd returned to the booth and saw that he was filling out a statement form.

"He wrote a grievance on me," Grant answered. "Can I put you down as a witness?"

****

Friday rolled around, and Shonda still hadn't heard from Mario. She'd been calling and leaving messages on his phone, but he hadn't responded. Yesterday, the operator informed her that his cell phone was disconnected. That revelation, plus the things that the guy told her in East Lake Meadows, had her thinking doubtfully. She wasn't in love with Mario, but it would be a lie if she declared she didn't have feelings for him. She just wished, she knew what he was involved in, and what she could do to get him out of it.

Well, it seemed as if she was about to get her wish because Mario was sitting on her porch when she arrived home. As she parked she grabbed her pocketbook and lunged from the car like a raging bull.

"Boy, what you done got into!" she demanded, now standing in front of Mario, who didn't bother standing up.

"What are you talking about?" he asked, innocently.

"Don't give me that shit, Mario!" she fussed. "I was in East Lake Monday. Somebody told me you stole from somebody." That's when she noticed the bookbag sitting beside him. "What's in the bookbag?"

"Clothes," he answered quickly.

Shonda was not going for it. Perhaps he sensed this, because he reluctantly unzipped the top, so she could see the clothes that looked as if they were just thrown into the bag.

That wasn't enough for her. "So, you ain't gon' tell me what's going on?"

"Can we go inside, first?" he asked. "It's cold out here!"

Shonda wanted to stand her ground a little longer, but it was, indeed cold, and her body temperature was dropping by the second. So, for the sake of her catching pneumonia, she gave in. Once, they were inside, Shonda punched in her alarm code, then turned the heat up on the thermometer. She, then, turned to Mario, thrusting her hands upon her hips.

"What?" he asked like he didn't know why she was giving him that look.

"Nigga, don't play with me!" Shonda snapped. "You either tell me what's going on, or get the fuck out of my house, and don't bring your ass back!"

"Baby, calm down!" Mario said, placing the bookbag on the sofa. "I'ma tell you everything. Right now, I'm hungry as hell! Can I eat first? I promise, when I finish eating, I'ma tell you everything you need to know."

"Well, I'm finna take a shower," she told him. "By the time I'm done, you should have a whole storybook full of lies to tell me."

Shonda stormed off to the bedroom and locked the door, just in case Mario thought he was going to catch her once she was undressed and fuck her until her brain cells were so low, she forgot about the situation at hand. She wouldn't deny that he had the ability to do it, but it wasn't going down like that, today! If he wanted some pussy – she damn sure wanted some dick – then, it would be after he told her what she needed to know. Then again, that depended on what he told her because, as far as she knew, he had done something that put, not only his but her life in danger, also.

As she undressed, she could hear Mario in the kitchen, messing up her dishes, which let her know he wasn't waiting outside the door for her, but she still exited the bedroom, quickly, and locked the bathroom door behind her. After adjusting the water temperature to her liking, she climbed in and stood under the shower head. The water was so soothing, she just closed her eyes and let the sensation overtake her.

For some reason, she started thinking about Sheila and Grant. She knew, eventually, Grant was going to seduce her cousin, which was funny, because, although Grant had a reputation for being a man whore at the jail, he and Sheila seemed like a nice pair. She just hoped they'd have fun on their date, tonight.

"Girl, you should come with us," Sheila had suggested.

"Nah, girl," Shonda declined. "This is y'all first date. Just have a good time and call me with all the details tomorrow. *All the details*.

Shonda was pulled from her reverie by the sound of the doorbell. She was so caught up in her abstract thinking, she didn't know that she had been lathering herself with body wash.

"See who that is, Mario!" she yelled, thinking it might be Sheila stopping by before meeting up with Grant.

Thinking this, she began rinsing off, feeling that Sheila may need a little pep talk, and didn't want to keep her cousin waiting. The doorbell rang again.

"Mario, see who's at the door!" she yelled again. "Mario?"

She turned off the water and listened while she dried off, but the house was quiet. Then, she thought she'd heard the front door open.

"Who is it, Mario?"

Getting no response, she wrapped the towel around her and exited the bathroom. Upon entering the living room, she expected to see Sheila. Instead, she was looking down the barrel of a gun.

CHAPTER 6

"What's going on?" Shonda asked.

"That's what we're trying to find out," the White male cop answered, lowering his gun, but not reholstering it. "Your alarm company called the police, reporting a possible break-in."

"A break-in!" That's when she remembered Mario.

A quick glance towards the kitchen showed he wasn't there. She also noticed his bookbag was no longer on the sofa.

"That was the call that came over the radio," he replied. "The alarm company said you were not answering your phone. This *is* your home, isn't it?"

"Of course, *this is my home!*" Shonda took offense.

"Okay, first, I need you to reset your alarm," he told her. Then, I'll need to see some identification."

Shonda knew it was policy, so, without a word, she closed the front door, reset the alarm, and headed for her bedroom with him close behind. After entering the room, she pulled her State ID and driver's license from her purse, and handed them to the officer, who looked them over, then handed them back.

"Do you have any idea why your alarm—"

"My boyfriend," she cut him off, checking her cell phone and seeing the alarm company had called her, twice.

"Your boyfriend?"

"Yeah," she answered. "He left after I got in the shower. I guess he forgot I had set the alarm."

"So, that would explain why your front door was unlocked," he summarized.

"Yes."

Once he'd radioed to the station that everything was 10-4, and told Shonda to have a nice day, she walked him to the door to let him out, but, as she was closing the door, she noticed something that caused her heart to drop to her stomach. Her car was gone!

****

"Did you have a good time?" Grant finally asked Sheila as they traveled the interstate in his gray Cadillac.

"I had a wonderful time!" she answered, smiling. "I can't remember the last time I've had that much fun."

"That's because you don't get out often," he told her. "You're too good looking to be cooped up in the house all day! Now, I've seen some women who should never come out of the house until Halloween!"

"That's not nice!" Sheila asserted but was laughing right along with him.

All day, Grant had, not once, failed to amuse her. Hell, he was more entertaining than the games at Dave and Buster's, but at the comedy club. He had to sit back and let the comedians do what they do best, which was okay with her because every laugh they'd shared, seemed to add to the chemistry she felt between them. It was just too bad the night was about to end. Or, was it?

"Should I walk you to your apartment?" Grant asked, after entering her apartment complex and parking.

"I would only expect that from a gentleman," she answered, looking into his eyes.

Catching the hint, he cut the engine, and they both dismounted, then walked side by side to her apartment. As they walked, Sheila was debating if she should give in to her hormones and force herself on him. Well, it really wouldn't be much of a force, because, during their date, she'd periodically catch him staring at her with lustful eyes. So, she was half-expecting him to come on to her, first.

"Well, this is it," he said when they reached the door.

"Is it?" Sheila asked, hearing the words, but not believing she'd actually said them.

Well, that did the trick, because Grant took that as his cue, and closed the gap between them. Sheila's coat was unbuttoned, so, when Grant's hands wrapped around her waist, the sensation caused her eyes to automatically close. Her lips parted as soon as his made contact with them. The kiss was so passionate, Sheila had forgotten how cold it was, until her feet betrayed her, causing her to pull back.

"Andrew—" she started.

"I came on too strong, huh?" he asked, taking a step back.

"No,' she answered, pulling out her keys. "It's freezing out here."

When they entered the apartment, Sheila went straight to the thermostat to activate the heating system, while Grant locked the door. When she turned around, she saw Grant was still standing by the door, looking like a lost child. Sheila had never been the initiator when it came to sex, but there was a first time for everything. So, allowing her hormones to take over, she walked over, grabbed him by the hand, and led him to the bedroom.

****

"I'll see you when I get home," Ebony told Charles, and bid Ms. Bernice and Eugene goodnight before crossing the church's parking lot with Shonda and Sheila, to Sheila's Kia Sportage.

It was Sunday, and Shonda could not believe she'd let Ebony drag her to church, to prove a point to Charles' mother, but what she really couldn't believe was that Mario had actually stolen her car. Friday, she'd given him the benefit of a doubt, thinking he had to handle some important business, and that he would be right back, but when she'd awakened, Saturday morning, and assessed the situation by putting two main clues together Mario's hazardous situation, and the bag of clothes she came to the conclusion that Mario may have used her car as a means to skip town.

Therefore, she had no choice but to report it stolen. She just didn't expect the same cop who'd showed up at her house on Friday, to show up, and she definitely didn't expect him to remember her car wasn't there on his last visit, or for him to be asking questions about her boyfriend, who'd triggered the alarm that prompted his arrival the previous day.

"What's his name?" the cop had asked.

"Mario Ballard," she answered, hoping like hell Mario didn't have any warrants out for his arrest.

"Is he the one who stole your car, Ms. Watson?"

"I don't know who stole my car," Shonda lied, hating she'd even made the call. "I just want the report filed."

The officer did the necessary paperwork, but Shonda was quite sure he'd pinned Mario as a cardinal suspect.

"Stop by Taco Bell first Sheila," Ebony said from the back seat, once they were all settled in. "I told Erica and mama that I would bring them some tacos."

"Sounds good to me!" Sheila asserted, pulling out of the parking lot.

"And why you ain't tell me about the hot date you had, Friday?" Ebony inquired. "Who is he?"

"Yeah, who is he, Sheila?" Shonda chimed in with a smirk on her face.

"His name is, Andrew," Sheila answered, trying to keep from blushing. "He works at the jail with us."

"I heard he took you to Dave and Buster's and a comedy club," Ebony added with an amusing tone.

"It sounds like you heard quite a lot," Sheila shot an accusing look over at Shonda.

"Everything but the details," Shonda countered, smiling.

"What details?" Now, Ebony was leaning forward between the front seats. "Girl, you finally gave that cooty-cat up?"

"We just got out of church, crazy girl!"

"The best time for a testimony," Ebony joked. "Now, confess them sins!"

Sheila hesitated, but she knew Ebony was not going to let up. Therefore, she gave up the raunchy details of her sexcapade with Grant. After they'd ordered from Taco Bell's drive-thru, they headed for Ebony's mother's house, where they all assembled in the living room to eat and conversate.

"Mama, why would you get a cat?" Ebony asked. "You're scared of cats."

"I'm not scared of cats, Ebony," her mother contradicted. "I just don't like 'em."

"Well, why would you get something you don't like?"

"To try something new," she answered. "You gotta try something new in your life, every once in a while."

"Mama, you need a man!" Erica intervened.

"I said, something *new,* " Ms. Davis countered. "Besides, a man should be the last thing on *your* mind, Cinderella!"

Erica scowled at her mother, which made everyone laugh.

"Mama, that's not nice!" said Ebony.

"But it's true, Erica should be concentrating on getting herself together. I shouldn't have to tell her that a man ain't nothing, but another problem added to her life."

"You can say that again!" Shonda voiced.

"And how did you let a man steal your car Shonda?" Ms. Davis asked.

"To be honest, I didn't even expect him to do something like that."

"Girl, you should always expect a man to do what a man is capable of doing," she advised.

Ebony's mother had asserted that statement to Shonda, but Sheila knew it was intended for all of them. For it definitely stuck in her head as she drove home, after dropping Shonda off and leaving Ebony at her mother's house, where she was having dinner, tonight.

It was only after 3:00 p.m. when Sheila returned home, and she did not plan on being alone for the rest of the day. So, after changing clothes, she called Andrew to see if he would come over and keep her company.

"I could swing through around seven if that's okay with you," he told her.

"I guess I don't have a choice," said Sheila.

"Should I bring dinner?"

"Nah," she answered. "I couldn't let you do that. You treated me on Friday. I can, at least, cook you, dinner. That should keep me busy until you get here."

"Okay," he agreed. "I can go for a home-cooked meal, tonight."

That did it, while Sheila set out to cook pork chops, macaroni and cheese, sweet corn, and rolls, she made a call to Shonda to check on her, and brag.

"You doing what!" Shonda exclaimed. "You ain't never cook for me heifer!"

"Don't even go there!" Sheila said, laughing.

"I'm jealous, right now!"

"I still love you, baby!"

"Whatever!" Shonda asserted. "You just make sure he don't have you too tired to get your butt up in the morning! And don't forget you gotta pick me up!"

"Girl, I ain't forgot."

Getting off the phone with Shonda, and waiting for the pork chops to thaw out, Sheila did a thorough investigation of her apartment to make sure everything was in order and up to par. She'd even lit some of her potpourri candles and put five R&B CDs into the stereo's changer. Andrew proved to be a man of his word. He showed up a few minutes before seven. They ate, conversated, and around eight-thirty, Sheila knew she had to get to bed, but she was not letting him leave without a dose of his magic stick. But, first, she had to wash dishes.

"Let me go in here and wash these dishes before it gets too late," she said, getting off the sofa they were both occupying.

Andrew caught her by the arm, pulling her back onto the sofa. "I'll handle that. You stay your fine ass right there!"

All Sheila could do was smile as she watched him make his way to the kitchen. She relished the way he'd taken charge, but she was not going to obey him, and just sit there. In fact, she was going to disobey him by being very naughty.

She eased off the sofa and entered her bedroom, where she stripped off all her clothes and slipped into a light-brown camisole. When she returned to the living room, she re-started *Usher's 'U Got It Bad,'* and sauntered into the kitchen, but Andrew was so busy with the dishes, he didn't notice her until she approached him from the side and pressed her body into his.

"Damn!" he exclaimed, taking a step back, getting an eyeful.

"Did I scare you?' she teased, standing akimbo.

He smirked, dried his hands on his pants and in a swift motion, lifted her up on the counter. This startled her a bit, but before she could catch her breath or her bare bottom adjusted to the cold countertop, Andrew was standing between her legs with his mouth on hers, delivering the best breath-taking kiss that had ever been bestowed upon her.

After a moment of lip locking, Andrew lifted her thighs until her feet were planted on the counter, which sent sharp pains through her joints, being that she had never been put in this position before. When Andrew's mouth made contact with her womanhood, and his tongue started touching places that had not been touched in centuries – well since Friday – the pain in her joints seemed to just fade away.

****

"Can you at least, be there before ten-thirty?" Ebony asked Erica, who was driving her home from their mother's house.

"I'll try," Erica said. "Like I said, I'm used to working at night, so it's gonna take a while for me to adjust to getting up that early, but I do need the money, so I'll try."

"That's the spirit!" Ebony said, smiling. "I already told mama to wake you up around nine-fifteen."

"Knowing her, it would probably be eight-fifteen," Erica mumbled.

"She's just not used to seeing you like this," said Ebony. "Neither am I. It's like you always had this certain glow about you. You paraded around like you were the Queen of England, and didn't care what anybody thought, or said about you. That's the Erica we remember. We want that Erica back."

Erica didn't respond, but Ebony knew what she said had hit home, and she was going to do whatever it took to help her sister get back on her feet.

"The next one," Ebony said as they approached her house, where her car was only car in the driveway.

"Girl, you're living the good life!" Erica said, pulling in behind Ebony's car. "You hit the jackpot, for real!"

"It's not even like that," Ebony countered.

"So, you don't really stay here?" Erica was being sarcastic. "That's not your brand-new Infiniti? You don't own a beauty salon?"

"It's all material," Ebony said, regarding the empty spot beside her car. "It comes and goes."

"Yeah, easy for you to say. A lot of women would kill to be in your shoes. To be who you are, to have what you have, and you know that, Ebony. So, don't sit there and act like you got it bad."

"It ain't always what it seems." Ebony leaned over and kissed her sister on the jaw. "I'll see you in the morning."

Entering the house, Ebony headed for her bedroom, undressed, and went to the bathroom to shower. As she showered, she could not help but wonder why Charles hadn't made it home yet. She had deliberately stayed out a little late to prove a point to him. Well, it seemed as if he was out to prove a point of his own.

It didn't matter to Ebony, because she had a few more tricks up her sleeves. One way or another, she was going to make him realize she was not going to neglect her friends for him or anybody else! After drying off and slipping into a pair of pajamas, she cleaned the tub, then retreated to the bedroom, where she placed the TV on mute before climbing into bed.

It was after nine, and she still couldn't believe Charles didn't have the decency to call and let her know he was okay.

'*Maybe this is part of his plan,*' she thought, grabbing the remote and surfing through the channels of the volume less television.

Before she could find something worth looking at, she heard the front door open and close, which was her cue to initiate Plan B. She placed the remote on the nightstand and pulled the covers over her head to fake like she was asleep. She listened as Charles entered the room and rummaged around. Seconds later, he left back out. She then heard the bathroom door close, indicating that he was about to take a shower, being that the bathroom adjacent to their bedroom didn't have a shower.

Ebony tried to stay awake long enough to see if he was going to try and see if she was awake and ask for sex, but she was so tired, she ended up drifting off to sleep, only to be awakened by her alarm clock. Silencing the alarm, she looked over to see Charles was still not in bed. It infuriated her to think that he'd chosen to sleep in another part of the house because he was too mad to sleep beside her, but after checking every room in the house, then peering out the window to see that his car was gone, she realized that may not have been the case.

His early and unannounced departure was enough for her to reconsider that thought because they would always leave the house, together, or a few minutes apart. So, it was patent that they had implicitly declared war.

"May the best man win!" she mumbled as she headed back towards the bedroom, but as she came upon the main bathroom, she had a notion to check the tub to see if Charles had left it dirty again. To her surprise, the tub was clean, but as she stood there, she was overwhelmed with the feeling that something was amiss, which made her survey the bathroom as if she would find a clue. That's when she noticed the clothes hamper was slightly turned from its normal position. She straightened it, with the intent to leave out and prepare for work, but her mind wouldn't allow it. Something was telling her to look inside the hamper.

Giving in to her thoughts, she lifted the lid to see her bra, and a pair of her panties, on top of one of Charles' tee shirts which were the only items, being that she had done the laundry on Saturday. She was about to let the top back down when realization kicked in. She had taken her shower before Charles, so her underwear should be *under* his shirt. Now, extremely curious, she picked her panties and bra up in one hand, then looked down at the shirt that was balled up as if something was inside of it.

At this point, she was feeling silly, not knowing what she was expecting to find until she lifted the shirt, and a pair of Charles' briefs tumbled out of it. This is where she started feeling guilty of betrayal, because here she was, snooping through the dirty clothes hamper like she'd lost trust in the man she'd promised to, someday, walk down the aisle with.

Whether it was true or not, she still found it strange that he had endeavored to conceal his underwear under hers. So, giving in to her basic instinct, she picked the briefs up, held them to her nose, and sniffed the crotch, inhaling the faint, undeniable scent of another woman.

CHAPTER 7

After their sexual romp, Andrew left, being that he also had to get up for work. Sheila couldn't wait to get to work, so she could spend all day with him, but her plans were deterred when Lieutenant Wilcox the shift supervisor for the day told her that she was assigned to five Southeast, dorm two hundred, with Shonda Watson.

"Girl, snap out of it!" Shonda said, nudging Sheila in the shoulder with her elbow.

"What?" replied Sheila, who'd been daydreaming about Andrew again.

"That nigga got you dick whipped!" Shonda accused. "And I thought Charles had Ebony fucked up!"

"Look who's talking!" Sheila stood her ground. "Don't get me started on you and *Mr. Grand Theft Auto!*"

Shonda laughed. "No, you didn't? That was a low blow, right there!"

"A well deserved low blow!" Sheila added, also laughing. "Speaking of whipped here comes your secret crush."

Shonda looked up to see the inmate who always stopped by the booth whenever he was out on free time. It was funny to her that she had been conversing with this guy and didn't even know his name.

"What's up, Bankhead!" Shonda regarded him by his locale, remembering he'd told her that he was from Bankhead Highway.

"I can't call it," he replied. "I see you got 'cha homegirl back."

"Just her body," Shonda joked. "I don't know where her mind is."

"Did she tell you she was now single?" Sheila asked Bankhead, taking the unwanted attention off herself.

"You and ol' boy broke up?" he asked Shonda.

"He walked out on her," Sheila answered for her. "Well, that was until he got to the driveway. Then he drove the rest of the way."

Shonda was laughing hysterically. "Sheila, I'ma kick your ass!"

****

"Can I go ahead and take a quick break, Boss Lady?"

Ebony had heard Pam's question, although her mind was elsewhere as she added extensions to the head of one of her customers. All day, she'd been mulling over the discovery she'd made, this morning. She couldn't believe Charles, Saint Charles was cheating on her. Now, she was anxious to know who the bitch was, and how long had this been going on."

"A quick break?" Ebony now regarded Pam, who was standing beside her.

"Like twenty or thirty minutes," replied Pam. "I know, I got two more clients, but I can finish with them by closing time. I just need to handle some very important business."

"That's really *your* decision, Pam," Ebony asserted. "You can stay out all week, but as long as you claim that chair, I want my money."

"Girl, you okay?"

"Yeah, I'm good," she lied. "Why you ask?"

"Cause you ain't acting like you today," Pam pointed out.

"Well, who am I acting like?" Ebony asked, trying her best to contain the anger that had been building up inside her all morning.

"You ain't acting like *you*!"

"I thought you had some business to take care of," Ebony huffed, hoping Pam would get the hint and stop probing.

Apparently, Pam had gotten the hint and stormed out of the store. Ebony knew everyone had witnessed the scene but didn't care to pay them any mind as she proceeded with her client's hair, but she knew that an apology to Pam was in order.

"I'm back," Erica said, upon entering the shop, returning from her break. "What 'cha got for me?"

"The restroom," Ebony answered.

"I did that, earlier."

Ebony had to think for a few seconds. She had pretty much run out of things for Erica to do. Then, she realized some of their customers' hair was to be shampooed and conditioned before being styled. "You feel like shampooing and conditioning?" Ebony asked her sister.

"Do I have a choice?"

"Not really," answered Ebony. "Khandi, could you get Erica set up for hair treatment?"

While Khandi tended to Erica, Ebony slipped back into her thoughts. Now, she was wondering if she should bring it to Charles' attention that she was aware of his infidelity or get even.

****

"Girl, you should get even with his trifling ass!" Shonda insisted, keeping her voice leveled, so she wouldn't be heard by the other people dining at the restaurant.

Ebony had called Shonda and Sheila at their job and asked them to meet her at Long John Silvers, around five-thirty, telling them it was important, and she would buy them dinner. She was reluctant to disclose her discovery to them, but she needed someone to confide in. She just wasn't ready to tell Erica, who would just take it to Charles' ass like a man, as she'd done to a lot of guys in school, whenever Ebony would complain of being mistreated.

"That's messed up!" Sheila asserted. "He's supposed to be a Christian!"

"Maybe we should go over there and baptize his ass!" Shonda offered.

"We'll just make it look like he fell asleep in the tub," Shonda continued.

"Shonda, would you stop!" Ebony protested.

"Hell no!" Shonda stood her ground. "That nigga hurt you, and he deserves to be hurt back!"

"Well, could you be more logical?"

"Not really."

"Please?"

That's when Shonda remembered that Ebony as well as Sheila and Theresa had always looked up to her, and valued her opinion, so, for her friend's admiration for her, she decided to maintain a leveled head, in order to give her logical advice.

"So, what do you wanna hear?" Shonda asked Ebony, after taking a deep breath.

"Anything that doesn't involve violence," answered Ebony.

"Okay." Shonda agreed. "He got him some outside pussy. Get you some outside dick."

"Two wrongs don't make it right!" Sheila interjected.

"But it'll make her feel better," Shonda countered. "Besides, I'm quite sure his fat ass ain't slinging dick like that. Hell, he probably don't even know what his dick looks like."

"So, you insist I do my thing too?" Ebony asked.

"Exactly!" Shonda answered. "Don't even say nothing to him about another bitch. Get all you can out of that dog, so if he decides to leave you for another bitch, you won't be too fucked up about it, because you got yours."

Ebony had asked Shonda to be logical, and she did. She didn't know if she was going to follow Shonda's advice, but she definitely pondered it on her drive home. She didn't even know if she could or even possessed the will to carry on around Charles as if nothing was amiss.

Well, she was about to find out, because, to her surprise, Charles was already home when she arrived, but she didn't expect for him to meet her at the door like he was on his way out.

"Hey, baby!" He greeted her with a peck on the cheek. "You hungry?"

"Um, yeah," she answered, baffled by his sudden change of attitude.

"I was gonna stop by the Rib Shack and grab us a plate," he told her.

"What, I can't go with you?" Ebony asked, figuring he was using this run as an excuse to get him a quickie.

"Of course, you can. I just figured you were tired and wanted to get off your feet."

"I'm okay," she said. "If you want to, we can take my car. I had the heat on, so the interior should still be warm."

****

A week had gone by, and either Charles was being extremely careful, or he'd relinquished his secret love affair because Ebony had been attentively snooping around for clues to no avail. She was starting to think, maybe he'd only stepped out on her that one time, which was fathomable to some degree. However, Ebony had yet to take Shonda's advice and got her some outside dick because everything seemed to be back to normal. Plus, they'd started back communicating verbally and sexually like they'd used to.

Now, Ebony was at work, trying to finish her second of three heads for today, so she could get home and freshen up. Today was Charles' birthday and she had made reservations at Justin's in Buckhead. Plus, she'd ordered a limousine and driver that would pick them up at the house.

"Ebony, can I borrow your curlers?" Coco, one of the stylists asked.

"Don't you have curlers?" Ebony regarded the tall, dark-complexioned stylist towering over her.

"They have a shortage in them," Coco told her. "It won't take long, I just have to do a bang."

"Don't make me hunt your tall ass down 'bout my curlers!" Ebony joked, handing over the curlers.

Seconds after Coco walked off, the sound of a car's sound system vibrated the store's front windows and caught everyone's attention. Everybody already knew who the occupant was in the blue Cadillac Escalade that parked right in front of the shop, which is why everyone's attention had shifted from the truck to Pam. Who'd proceeded with her customer's hair like she hadn't noticed Ted, her on-and-off boyfriend, had pulled up.

Ted from what Pam had contributed to the gossip column was heavy in the drug game, but couldn't keep his dick in his pants, which was why they would periodically undergo temporary break-ups. Each time, Pam would swear she was through with him.

"Pam, can I holler at you outside for a minute?" Ted inquired, only sticking his head in the door.

Again, everyone shifted their attention to Pam, who still tended to her client's hair like she was deaf and unaware of what was going on.

"Pam, you need to handle that!" Ebony prompted. "And Ted, you need to understand that this is a place of business. This is her job, bringing drama to her workplace can get her fired."

"Nah, it ain't like that, Ms. Ebony," Ted assured. "I came in peace. I just need to speak with her for a minute, but I apologize for the inconvenience.

Once again, all eyes were on Pam. She smacked her lips, apologized to her client, then marched out of the shop, where she and Ted stood out front to settle their differences.

"Can anybody read lips?" Khandi asked, prompting laughter from the other girls.

"For real!" Coco chimed in. "We need to put a call box by the door, so we can hear the drama in Hi-Definition!"

"Y'all ain't right!" Ebony asserted, laughing right along with them.

"So, that's Ted, huh?" asked Erica, who was now standing beside Ebony, wearing rubber cleaning gloves.

The inflection of Erica's voice which was perceivably amusing abruptly ended Ebony's laughter, causing her to regard Erica with a grave look. Erica didn't see the look, because she was too busy admiring Ted, and Ebony was familiar with the look in Erica's eyes.

She had always revered her sister for how she would set her sights on something and would stop at nothing to conquer it, but right now, was not one of those times.

"Erica!" Ebony waved her hand in Erica's face, getting her attention. "Don't even think about it!"

****

"How long a drive is that?" Shonda asked Sheila, who was, once again on post with her.

Yesterday, upon leaving work, Shonda checked the messages on her cell phone to see that she had received one from Chatham County Police Department, informing her that they had recovered her car, and she had to come down and fill out the necessary paperwork for it to be released to her.

Shonda was not expecting this. She was really expecting to hear that Mario had tried to cross the Mexico border in her car. Now, she was sure he was locked up at the Chatham County Jail, which was where he was going to stay because she was not going to donate a quarter of a penny towards his bond.

"I don't know," Sheila answered her question. "But for some reason, I feel like I'm bound to find out."

"Girl, you know I'ma need you to drive me down there," Shonda asserted.

"How much are you gonna charge me?"

"Just pay for the gas and buy me dinner."

Shonda smiled. "Oh, I can buy you dinner. Just don't be stingy with the booty when we get to the hotel."

"Sounds like you plan on taking me to Italy for dinner," Sheila jokingly flirted back.

"Damn, you got some expensive booty!"

While they were laughing from the witty comment, the buzzer sounded on the panel. That's when they spotted Lieutenant Mallery and a male Captain in the sally port.

"Are you gonna buzz the witch in?" Shonda asked, seeing the evil look in Sheila's face, which she found funny.

"Only because she got the Captain with her," Sheila replied, buzzing them in.

Mallery sashayed up to the booth, with the Captain at her heels. Feeling as if Mallery was there to sign the logbook, Shonda handed it to her, in which Mallery just looked at, before telling her to conduct a security check.

Shonda didn't hesitate. She left the booth, starting on the bottom range, where the inmates were locked in their cells, being that the top range was out on their free time. As she made her rounds, she kept an eye on the activity at the booth. She saw Mallery hand Sheila a piece of paper, in which Sheila began writing on.

"Ms. Watson!" an inmate called her as she was passing one of the cells. Stopping in her tracks, she looked to see Bankhead's face in the rectangular-shaped window of the door. "What do you need, sir?" she asked, assuming formality for the sake of her guests.

"Shit, a down-ass chick!" he answered.

"I'll see if I have one when I get back to the booth," she answered, annoyed at the fact that he didn't see that now was not the time.

She cleared the bottom range and climbed the stairs to the top range, taking another glance at the desk, but thinking of Bankhead. It was no doubt that he was trying to get at her, but she was not going down that road again.

Lieutenant Mallery and the Captain had already left by the time Shonda had made it back to the booth. She signed the logbook before asking Sheila of the supervisors' visit.

"They wanted me to write a statement for Grant," Sheila answered, then told her about the grievance an inmate had filed on him for assault.

"Damn!" Shonda exclaimed. "You got it like that?" Maybe I *will* take you to Italy for a piece of that booty!"

****

Ebony had managed to leave the salon, shortly after three, leaving Khandi in charge of locking up. She had also told Erica she could leave after she'd completed her list of chores. Ebony arrived home and saw that Charles had not made it in yet, although she'd told him, yesterday that she needed him home around four because she was taking him out for his birthday. It was only three-thirty, and the limousine was scheduled to arrive in an hour. So, instead of worrying, she proceeded to tend to get herself ready.

After the twenty-something minute shower, Ebony headed for the bedroom to dry off and apply her cosmetics. Still, Charles had not made it in. Now, she was starting to worry, so after donning the dress and heels she'd bought for the occasion, she dialed his cellular, which took him longer than usual to answer.

"I know, I know," he answered, evidently checking the caller ID, beforehand. "I'm with a client, right now. As soon as I close this deal, I'll be on the way."

"Okay," was all Ebony could say before he abruptly hung up.

Ebony didn't let that bother her, because she was determined she was going to enjoy herself, tonight. Besides, she had never been to Justin's, which is why she'd chosen the restaurant. So, although this was Charles' day, she was going to enjoy herself and her money as well.

Being that the limousine wasn't expected for another thirty minutes, Ebony gave herself a last-minute inspection, then entered the living room. She sat in the recliner to watch TV and await Charles' arrival, but she ended up dozing off, only to be awakened by the sound of the doorbell. As she half-staggered towards the door, she glanced at her watch to see that it was four thirty-five.

"Who is it?" she asked, not tall enough to access the peephole.

"Limousine service," a male's voice resounded.

Ebony opened the door to a well-dressed guy, who she immediately noticed was very handsome perhaps too handsome to be a chauffeur.

"I was blowing the horn," said the man, who looked to be in his early forties. "Are you ready?"

"My husband isn't here yet," she answered, feeling a bit flustered. "He should be here shortly," she added.

"Alright, I'll be in the car."

The driver turned and headed for the white, stretch Lincoln Town car parked in front of the house, which Ebony had taken a moment to admire before closing the door and retreating to the living room. She retrieved her cell phone off the table to call Charles, but this time, he wasn't answering.

Trying again, and getting the same results, she called his office phone, only to get the answering machine. She could not believe this was happening. Charles had never refused to answer his phone. Now, she was beginning to think something was wrong. Well, of course, something was wrong, but not being able to pinpoint exactly what is what bothered her.

Not knowing what to do at the moment, Ebony retook her seat in the recliner and thought about how today was already looking like a disaster. It's not even her birthday, but the fact that she had put forth the time and effort to plan something special for him, and he not have the decency to make sure he was on time, really infuriated her.

The more she thought about it, the angrier she'd become, but she couldn't help it. Now, she was to the point where she'd started panting and fighting back tears. She was preoccupied with her thoughts until they were interrupted by the sound of a car's horn. Half-thinking it was Charles, she bolted from the chair, marched to the front door, and snatched it open, but there was no Charles. It was only the chauffeur, who was standing outside the car, giving her an inquiring look.

This caused her to check her watch to see that it was a few minutes after five. Then, with her cell phone in hand, she dialed Charles' number again, to no avail, which almost caused her to slam the device into the floor, but instead, she held a finger up to the driver, as if telling him to hold on, before heading for the bedroom.

Ebony didn't know what she was about to do, but she knew she was not about to stay in that house, alone, when she had a limousine and a reserved table waiting for her at a fancy restaurant. After donning her overcoat, grabbing her pocketbook, and activating the alarm, she was out the door and headed for the limousine. The driver was waiting to open the door for her. She just hoped like hell he didn't ask about her husband, which would probably get him cursed out.

"Sorry to keep you waiting," she apologized.

"It's not your fault," the driver replied, opening the door for her. "He's the one that should be sorry."

Ebony was about to climb into the car, but his statement caused her to stop in her tracks and look him in his face, which was friendly and soothing, with eyes that regarded her with a warm look, despite the cold weather.

"I'm supposed to take you to Justin's, right?" he asked, drilling his eyes into hers, which made her heart flutter.

****

Sheila and Shonda had made the long drive to Savannah, Georgia, which took almost four hours, to find out that the impound was closed, except for the receiving department, where an older Black man occupied a small, cluttered desk.

"She didn't tell you that you had to pick up your car before five?" the man asked Shonda.

"No," she answered, pissed off that the receptionist bitch hadn't mentioned anything about closing time. "I told her, I was coming down today, once I got off work."

"Let me check the logbook," he said retrieving the book from under a mountain of documents and scanning it. "Name?"

"Shonda Watson."

"Ford Mustang, convertible, red in color?"

"That's it."

"I guess I'm authorized to sign it over to you," he asserted, handing her a clipboard containing forms. "First, you'll have to fill these out."

It took less than ten minutes for Shonda to fill out the paperwork and return them to the man, who signed them, then insisted they follow him. They followed him outside, where they passed rows of impounded vehicles until they came upon Shonda's car. Had it not been for the familiar license plate, she would have argued the man up and down that he had the wrong car, but the red Ford Mustang that sat before them on no tires, was, indeed, her car.

"Who stole the tires?" she inquired through clenched teeth.

"I assume the person that stole the car," the guy answered.

"Did they catch the person?" Shonda was so angry, she was actually seeing visions of her wringing Mario's neck.

"I don't know about anybody being caught," the man answered. "You'll have to get that information from the police department."

"So, how am I supposed to get this car home?"

"I have no idea, ma'am."

"Y'all don't have any spare tires laying around?" Sheila asked.

"Nope."

"What about a tire shop?" asked Shonda. "Is there one close by that would still be open?"

Finally, the old fart had become useful, by giving them directions to a tire shop that didn't have an exact closing time, and lucky for them, the place was still open, with one customer, who appeared to be getting a new pair of rims on his orange '79 Chevy Impala. Dismounting, Shonda and Sheila approached the tire man who was tending to the Chevy. He stopped what he was doing.

"We ain't order no strippers in police uniform," he spoke, regarding their work uniforms. "So, I assume y'all need some work done."

"I need to buy some tires," Shonda said, not in the mood for games.

"I can't help you with that today," he answered. "Once I finish with this customer, I'm closing down shop."

"Man sell them women some tires, Bubba!" asserted some tall, dark-skin guy who exited the shop, sprinkling marijuana into a blunt wrap.

"You know I'm trying to get home, derrty," said the tire man. "They can come back through tomorrow. The shop will still be in the same place."

"Not if I burn this bitch down!" the customer joked. "I know you're not gonna turn down these fine young women, so you can go home and watch reruns of *Hangin' with Mr. Cooper*."

"Why can't they just come back tomorrow?"

The customer turned to them. "Y'all can't come back tomorrow?"

Seeing that Shonda was already fed up, Sheila took the initiative, and explained the situation to them, leaving out the fact that they knew the person who'd stolen Shonda's car.

"That's fucked up!" the tall guy exclaimed, using his lighter to dry the blunt he'd just rolled up. "They drove all the way from that city, Norman. You gotta fuck wit 'em!"

"Yeah, I know," Norman said, standing. "That means I'll have to put your shit on hold, while I look for some tires."

"Man fuck that car!" the customer said. "I ain't got nowhere to go. I'm finna smoke this blunt and talk some shit."

"What kind of car is it?" asked Norman.

"Ford Mustang," Shonda told him.

"Shit, they call me, Doolu," the tall guy asserted. "Y'all smoke?"

Sheila wasn't a smoker, but Shonda was in dire need of some herbal relaxation at the moment, so while waiting for Norman to return, Shonda and Doolu enjoyed the blunt, and made small conversation. Sheila retreated back to her car, perhaps to avoid the cold air.

"You're too fine not to have a nigga," Doolu told Shonda.

"Niggas don't wanna act right."

"But all niggas ain't the same baby."

"Maybe not."

"I'll tell you what," he said, taking a long drag on the blunt. "Shoot me your number, I'll show you that all niggas ain't the same. Real shit!"

"How 'bout you give me *your* number?" Shonda asked, still mad at all men at the moment, and not sure if she was ready to get involved with another one.

****

"So, how long have you been a chauffeur?"

Ebony had planned to dine alone, but by the time they reached the restaurant, she was having second thoughts. She knew the place would be packed, and people would see her sitting alone and think she was stood up by her man which was the obvious truth. Therefore, she no longer possessed the courage to do what she had initially planned to do, but when the chauffeur opened the door for her, she assumed the same posture she had when she'd gotten into the car.

"What time will you be coming out?" he had asked.

"Don't you mean *we?*" Ebony asked, feeling as though she had taken on Erica's persona, which pretty much seemed appropriate at the time. "Park the car, I'll see you inside. Just tell them you're, Mr. White."

Then, without waiting for a response, she marched into the restaurant and was escorted to her table. Of course, she didn't think the chauffeur was actually going to join her, until moments later, he was escorted to the table. Now, they were enjoying dinner and a second bottle of champagne in which Ebony had consumed most of as they talked.

"I'm a surrogate chauffer," he now answered her question. "The driver who was assigned to you came down with the flu."

"Aww that's too bad," Ebony cooed, feeling the champagne working on her as she tried to decide if she should finish her steak and potatoes. "So, that's how you ended up stuck with me, huh?"

"It comes with the business."

"You still haven't told me your name."

"I'm Mr. White for the night," he answered with a grin on his face.

Ebony couldn't help but laugh. "And who will you be tomorrow?"

Before he could answer, a waitress approached and whispered in her ear, asking if she was ready for the cake, which caught her off guard because she had completely forgotten about the red velvet cake, she'd pre-ordered yesterday.

"Yes, I'm ready for it," Ebony answered, looking over at the driver, feeling a little guilty that Charles' cake was about to be handed to another man.

'*Oh, well,*' she thought, because how she was feeling right now, Charles' cake may not be the only thing handed to another man, tonight.

The waitress cleared their dishes before leaving the table. Moments later, the waitress, carrying the cake with thirty-five lit candles, and accompanied by some of her co-workers, approached singing the *Happy Birthday* song, which Ebony did not expect. Plus, they were singing the song to 'Charles," being that his name was on the cake.

When they surrounded the table, still singing, and placed the cake in front of the chauffeur, Ebony noticed he was regarding her with a stunned look. That she found extremely funny, but in lieu of laughing, she tilted her head to the side as if telling him to play his part. Acknowledging the look, he quickly assumed the biggest, plausible smile she'd ever seen simulated.

"I think this is the part where you blow out the candles," Ebony stated, once the song was over, prompting laughter from the quartet.

"How about I let you do the honors?" he asked.

"It's not my birthday," she replied, thinking he was going to say the same, but instead, he blew the candles out. Then, once handed the knife, he cut and served the first piece to Ebony.

"Thank you, sweetheart!" Ebony prompted with a broad smile, for the sake of the staff and the other diners who seemed to be enjoying the small spectacle at this particular table.

"Should I package it for you to take home with you?" their waitress asked the driver, who then shot Ebony an inquisitive look.

"No need to," Ebony bailed him out. "You can serve the rest to the other diners and thank you all so much!"

Playa Ray

CHAPTER 8

Ebony was awakened by the sound of someone knocking on the door. Once her eyes had adjusted, she noticed she was not at home, but in an expensive-looking hotel room. She threw the covers off her, seeing that she was still fully dressed, with the exception of her shoes.

Forgetting about the knock on the door that had awakened her, Ebony tried to retain the events of last night that had resulted in her waking up in a hotel room. She vividly remembered enjoying the cake and more conversation with the chauffeur, who'd insisted that she slow down on the champagne, but disregarding his suggestion, she ordered a third bottle. The last thing she remembered was him escorting her across the parking lot to the limousine.

Another knock on the door brought her out of her reverie, startling her a bit. Not knowing where she was, or who was at the door, she was in the least hurry to answer it.

Until someone beyond the door asserted, "Ms. Davis, your ride is here."

Hearing her name was enough for her to climb out of the huge bed, and pad across the soft carpet to the door where she opened it, thinking it was the chauffeur.

"Good morning!" a dark-skinned, butler-dressed man greeted, handing her a white, letter-sized envelope with Ms. Davis handwritten on it. Disregarding his greeting, she tore open the envelope and read the typed letter:

Ms. Davis,

Thank you for a wonderful evening! It's not every day that a beautiful woman forces me to have dinner with her and insist that it's my birthday. Anyway, you were beyond intoxication, and I didn't think it was wise to return you to your husband in such a state. Well, I'm sure you're sober now, so, once you get yourself together, Mr. Miller will drive you home. P.L.

"How long will you need, ma'am?" Mr. Miller sounded impatient.

"Not long," she answered, intentionally slamming the door in his face.

Getting back to the bed, she saw that her purse and heels were on top of the nightstand. Donning the heels, she grabbed her purse and headed for the bathroom, rummaging through it to make sure everything was still there. Everything seemed to be intact, so getting to the bathroom, she pulled out her small bottle of mouth wash and rinsed her mouth out. Once she was sure she was public ready, she made her exit.

Mr. Miller, who appeared to be in his late forties, was still standing in the hallway when she exited the room. "This way," was all he'd said, and led the way.

They rode the elevator in silence. Getting to the ground floor and out the front door, Mr. Miller opened the rear door of a black stretched Lincoln Town Car that was waiting in front of the building.

Ebony glanced around before climbing inside, and nothing looked familiar to her. She couldn't even see the name of the hotel, for the marquee they were under. Once inside the car, she looked at her wrist to check the time, but her watch was gone. That's when she noticed she was no longer wearing her necklace and earrings. Panicking, she rummaged through her purse, finding the items in the interior side pouch. While reapplying her jewelry, she tried hard to remember being brought to the hotel and taking off her shoes and jewelry but couldn't.

Now, she was wondering if 'P.L.' had taken those things off, and if so, what else had he done to her while she was as he put it beyond intoxication. She didn't know him from a can of paint, but, clearly, Mr. Miller did. Ebony wanted to ask him, but she didn't want him to think she'd had a one-night stand with a man, whose name she had no knowledge of.

Dismissing that thought, she checked her watch, seeing that it was ten minutes before eleven. She didn't worry about the running of the salon, because Khandi had the keys, and was reliable when it came to opening on time and making sure things were running well.

As the owner, Ebony felt she still had to call in and let her staff know if she was coming in or not.

She pulled her cell phone from her purse and saw that she only had one missed call, which was from Erica. It kind of irked her to see that Charles didn't even take the initiative to call and check on her. For all he knew, she could have been abducted from their very home, raped, murdered, and laying somewhere in a ditch. Just the thought of Charles not caring if something like that happened to her, caused her to break down and cry uncontrollably, not knowing, or even caring if Mr. Miller could hear her.

****

"Girl, I swear I don't wanna drive that car no more!" Shonda told Sheila as they exited the Dekalb County Jail, heading for their cars.

"It just don't feel the same, huh?" Sheila asked, knowing Shonda was still upset about her rims and sound system.

"If it wasn't for the fact that James had bought it for me," Shonda started, "I would drive it to a deserted road and set it on fire! Speaking of fire, Mario done burned his last bridge with me. That's on everything!"

"Calm down, baby," Sheila placed her hand at the small of Shonda's back. "Don't let it get you upset. I know it's hard not to but being mad won't change nothing."

They'd made it to Shonda's car that sat on four, black donut-looking spare tires, which the tire man claimed were the only tires he had for her particular car.

"Do I need to follow you home?" Sheila asked in a semi-joking matter, seeing the strange way Shonda was eyeing her car.

"I really don't feel like going home, right now," Shonda answered in a distant tone, not taking her eyes off the car.

"Well, where do you wanna go?" Sheila did not like the tone of her cousin's voice at the moment. "It's too cold for any outdoor activities, but if you got something in mind, I'm with you. Or, we can go and kick it at Ebony's shop, and catch up on the latest gossip.

I'm quite sure those late-night comedians will cheer you up. Especially Coco, with her crazy butt!"

"Yeah, that might work," Shonda said, sounding doubtful.

"I'll follow you," Sheila told her, then headed for her car, feeling like she was about to freeze to death.

Her Kia Sportage was raggedy, but the heater was highly reliable, which never took long to kick in. By the time they reached the expressway, the interior of her car was so hot, she had to turn the heat off and crack a window. At this moment, her cell phone rang. Keeping her eyes on the busy road, she answered it, not checking the caller ID.

"You should be on your way home by now, huh?" Andrew's voice came in on the other end.

"I should be," she answered, happy to hear from him, being that he was off today, and they hadn't talked since last night. "But I'm not, I'm on my way to my friend's salon."

"So, you don't know how long you'll be out?"

"Not really."

He was quiet.

"What's up?" she asked, sensing there was something he wanted to say.

"I, um…," he hesitated, then sighed. "Just call me when you get a chance."

"Is everything okay?" she asked, only to hear the sound of him hanging up on the other end.

Sheila sensed something was wrong but pushed the thought to the back of her mind. She could only deal with one patient at a time. The girls parked their cars in the parking lot of the plaza and entered the salon. Only to be told by Erica, who was lounging in Ebony's chair, that Ebony called, saying that she didn't feel too well, and wasn't coming in today. Being that Ebony had never taken a day off since she'd opened the salon, Shonda called her cell to make sure everything was well with her friend. Getting no answer, she and Sheila decided to drive out to her house, where Ebony's car was the only car in the driveway. Parking in front of the house, they dismounted and approached the front door.

"I hope she ain't got the flu," Sheila said, ringing the doorbell. "That's my girl and all, but I can't afford to get sick right now."

"Hell, we both can't afford to get sick," Shonda agreed. "But if she needs nursing, and Charles won't do it, that's a chance we'll have to take."

Sheila rung the bell again. After another moment of waiting, Shonda tried the knob, seeing that the door was unlocked, they exchanged glances for a split second before Shonda took it upon herself to enter, followed by Sheila, who closed and locked the door.

"Girl, you know we can't be in here like this!" Sheila whispered. "What if the alarm—"

"It's not on," Shonda cut her off.

They exchanged a more serious glance this time. Sheila didn't know what to think or do, but she was right on the heels of Shonda, who had started tiptoeing through the house. It didn't take long for them to find Ebony's bedroom, where she was lying atop her bed in a blue evening dress, with her face buried in her pillow. Seeing this, they quietly entered, approaching her side of the bed.

"Ebony?" Shonda whispered.

Ebony responded by slowly turning her head to face them, revealing teary red eyes.

"What's wrong, baby?" Shonda asked, taking a seat on the edge of the bed, placing a hand on Ebony's back as Sheila dropped to her knees, holding one of Ebony's hands.

"He don't love me no more," she managed, going into another crying spell.

All they could do was listen to her cry. Once she'd gotten it all out of her system. Sheila retrieved her a bottle of water, and they listened as she gave them the summary of yesterday and this morning.

"I thought you said everything was going well," Shonda said, once Ebony had finished.

"I guess I was fooled," she stated, sadly.

"I can't believe he stood you up like that," said Sheila, who was now leaning against the dresser. "You did all that for his birthday, and he wouldn't even spend it with you? He, of all people, should know God don't like ugly!"

" Man, I'm so sick of these niggas!" Shonda vented. "We need to start doing them like they do us! They shouldn't be able to hurt us, and we not hurt them back."

"I agree," said Sheila.

"I'm on some nigga hating shit, now!" Shonda stood, looking from her cousin to her friend. "I don't know about y'all, but it's Friday. I'm stressed, and I need some excitement tonight! Do anybody care to hit the club with me, later?"

"I'm in," Sheila said, only because she felt Shonda was going to get into it with someone tonight, perhaps a man.

"Ebony, you should join us," Shonda insisted. "Don't give that nigga the pleasure of knowing he hurt you. Once he sees that he can torment you, mentally, he'll repeatedly use it against you. You gotta play a sucker to catch a sucker."

****

Ebony didn't expect to be hit with one of *Robert Greene's 48 Laws of Power*, but Shonda was right. She was not going to give Charles the pleasure of knowing he'd hurt her. She was going to put up a front until she came up with a way to get him back for what he'd done.

After her friends left, Ebony, rejuvenated by Shonda's pep talk, took on a new attitude. She showered, redressed, cleaned the house, and ate two peanut butter and jelly sandwiches. She would cook, but Charles was picking up Robyn, today, and they would always bring home the family meal from Kentucky Fried Chicken.

It was well after five when Ebony had consumed her snack, and truth be told, she was really anticipating Charles' arrival, so she could show him the new her. Plus, she had donned a pair of her old jeans that showed off her curves. She was glad she didn't throw them away when Charles had voiced his opinion about her wearing inappropriate attire. Instead, she just kept them in the closet in the guestroom, where she kept all of her inappropriate gear, such as the leopard-skin, kitten-heel boots she had on, with the matching long-sleeved shirt that bared her cleavage.

Charles showed up with Robyn, a little after six, while Ebony was sitting on the bed, talking to Erica on the phone, telling her that everything was fine, and she didn't come in because she was exhausted.

"Girl, my man just got in," Ebony asserted, playing her part. "I'll talk to you later." Hanging up, she headed for the kitchen, ready to make her debut as the new and improved Ebony Davis.

"Hey, Auntie Ebony!" Robyn, who was seated at the kitchen table, beamed.

Ebony kissed her on the jaw. "Hey, sweetheart!" You brought, Auntie Ebony, some chicken?"

"My daddy brought all of us some chicken," she answered, watching her dad as he divided the food on three paper plates.

"So how was your day, baby?" Ebony asked kissing him on the jaw.

"It was, um," he stammered, a surprised look was on his face. "It was okay. How was yours?"

"Wonderful!" she replied, seeing the way he was regarding her body before she'd taken a seat beside Robyn. "What about you, Robyn, learn anything new, today?"

"My teacher let us make stuff out of clay," she answered, cheerfully.

"Really?" Ebony was so animated she couldn't tell if she was faking or not. "We made stuff out of clay when I was in school. I made an ashtray for my dad. What did you make?"

"I made a zebra," she answered. "My teacher said it looks like a cow."

"Now, how did your teacher get a zebra mistaken for a cow?"

"I don't know," answered Robyn, laughing at the funny look Ebony was giving her.

As they ate, Ebony maintained conversation with Robyn, and would periodically catch Charles getting an eyeful of her cleavage, which she'd taken the time to dash a little baby oil on, to give her breasts that prominent look that would keratinize a blind man.

After dinner, Ebony tended to the discarding of their disposable dishes, while Robyn took her bath, and Charles headed for the bedroom to prepare for his bath. By the time Charles had taken his bath, Ebony and Robyn were both curled up on the living room sofa, watching a movie and eating microwaved popcorn. Ebony wasn't at all surprised when he decided not to join them, claiming he needed to rest his back, and retreated to the bedroom. She just hoped he wasn't hinting that he wanted sex, because he was in for a big disappointment, tonight.

"It's time for bed, baby," Ebony told Robyn, once the movie ended. "Go and say goodnight to your, daddy."

Ebony waited outside of their bedroom until Robyn came out, then escorted her to her room to tuck her in.

"Don't forget to say your prayers," Ebony reminded, planting a kiss on Robyn's cheek.

"Okay."

Saying good night, Ebony entered their bedroom, where Charles was lying on his back with his shirt off, the covers pulled up to his waist, and his hands interlocked behind his head. Clearly, he knew she was on her way after tucking Robyn in and was expecting to get laid, but the thought of his fat ass touching her, right now made her cringe.

Ebony made a b-line to the adjacent bathroom to apply eyeliner. It was a few minutes after nine, and she'd promised to pick the girls up around ten, but time seemed to be moving too slow, and she was extremely anxious to get out of that house. That's when she figured she would leave early and hang out at Shonda's house until they were ready to hit whatever club Shonda had in mind.

She exited the bathroom and went to the closet, where she pulled a small black box from the top shelf that contained the gold Embassy watch she'd bought Charles for his birthday and handed it to him.

"Happy Birthday," she managed, then went over to her dresser to rummage through her panoply of perfumes.

"Thank you," she heard him say, but didn't reply as she donned some *Curves* body spray, then a pair of gold earrings. "You going somewhere?" he finally asked.

"I'm going out with my friends," she asserted, boldly, as she put on her waist-length leather coat.

She was half-expecting him to protest, but, instead, he just lied there with a skeptical look plastered over his face, which made Ebony feel like she was finally in control.

Playa Ray

CHAPTER 9

Two Months Later

I need to hurry up and trade this raggedy piece of junk in!" Sheila said to herself as she attempted to start her car for the third time.

She was already in a bad mood, which she credited to menstruation. Plus, she was being as patient as she could with Andrew, who had moved in with her three weeks ago. After being suspended without pay, two months prior, until the grievance pending against him was settled. He claimed to be out searching for a job, daily, but whenever Sheila returned home from work, he was always there.

The sound of a car's horn pulled her out of her reverie. It was Shonda, who'd pulled up in front of her. She held her hands up as if asking what's the problem. Sheila turned the ignition again, and the car's engine came alive. She gave the thumbs up to Shonda, who waved and drove out of the parking lot. Sheila gave her car another five minutes to warm up before pulling out.

When she entered her apartment, Andrew was sitting on the living room sofa with his feet propped up on the table, watching cartoons, and consuming a large bag of Cheese Puffs. He was unshaven, and his hair looked like it hadn't seen a comb since they were invented. Most women were intrigued by rough-looking men. Well, if that was the case then Andrew was definitely up for grabs because what she was looking at right now, was in no way alluring to her.

"Did you even look for a job today?" Sheila asked, now standing between him and the TV.

"I looked in the Classifieds," he answered, nodding at the newspaper that cluttered the coffee table.

"And?"

"I ain't seen nothing," he told her. "I'll try back with the police department tomorrow."

"Well, in the meantime. You need to clean up my apartment!" she asserted. "Don't let me come home to this again, Andrew!"

She stormed off towards the bedroom to prepare for a long, hot bath. She was hoping Andrew was smart enough to take heed to what she'd said, because, if not, he was going to have to shack up with one of his other hoes.

****

Shonda didn't know why, after all this time, she still expected to see Mario sitting on her front porch, every time she pulled up to her house. She still wanted to kick his ass for sabotaging her car, although she had managed to cop a set of used Ford Mustang tires and a factory based stereo system.

Mario had cost her a lot of money since they'd been dating, but she could not deny she still had strong feelings for him. She'd called Chatham, Fulton, and the Dekalb County Jails to see if he had been arrested and housed in their facilities, he wasn't. According to the Atlanta Police Department, there hadn't been an arrest of anyone by the name of Mario Ballard.

Shonda just hoped nothing bad had happened to him, considering what she'd found out when she drove to East Lake Meadows, looking for him. She still didn't know what he was caught up in, or what he'd run off with. Something inside her was telling her to drive out to East Lake, find the guy who'd informed her about it, and see if she could squeeze a little more information out of him.

Shonda entered East Lake Meadows and drove around to the spot where she had encountered the guy on her last visit. Again, the local drug dealers were standing around, waiting to make a sale, which is why Shonda felt they were now regarding her car to see if she was a customer or the police.

It didn't take her long to spot the guy in the crowd, who was wearing a long, black trench coat and skull cap. She was hoping he would just take the initiative and walk over, but he looked as puzzled as the rest of his homies. Then, she realized how different her car looked without the chrome wheels.

As much as she detested these projects, she knew she was going to have to step out of the car, so he could recognize and acknowledge her. Before she could release the latch on her seatbelt, he was making his way towards her car. Once he'd made it to the driver's side, she cracked the window a bit, allowing the cool November air in.

"I didn't get your name the last time," she told him.

"Neither did I get yours," he replied, looking around.

"Shonda."

"Trent."

"So, what's the word on, Mario?" she asked.

"We ain't heard nothing on him."

She hesitated before asking: "What happened?"

Trent just looked at her.

"I just wanna know if this could be resolved," she added, hoping he would give in.

"You shouldn't get involved," Trent finally spoke in a quiet tone. "I told you these people don't want money. They want your boyfriend's head on a platter and trust me, they got a price on his head that God Himself couldn't turn down!"

****

"Girl, where'd you get that pretty coat from?" Ebony finally asked Erica about the expensive-looking, black leather coat with the fur-trimmed hood she'd been wearing for two weeks now.

It was after five-thirty, and the other stylists had already left for the day. Ebony and Erica had done the last minute clean up and were on their way out.

"A friend bought it for me," Erica answered, pulling the hood over her head as they exited.

"What friend?" Ebony asked, locking the door. She didn't recall Erica mentioning anything about a *friend*.

"It's nothing serious, he's just a friend."

"There you go!" Ebony voiced, not wanting her sister to go down that same road, or one similar.

"It's nothing serious, Ebony," she restated, crossing the parking lot to their mother's car.

Ebony couldn't help but look at her butt, glad to see her sister's body had reclaimed the thickness the women in their family were known for. When she made it home, Charles met her at the front door, helping her out of her coat. Ever since she'd started hanging out with her friends on a regular and staying out late. Charles had been bending over backward and catering to her like he was vying for her attention. He'd even been showering her with gifts, such as flowers, cards, candy, and stuffed animals. Ebony knew he was only trying to wheel her back to the same Ebony she was two months ago, so he could have her wrapped around his fingers again. That was not going to happen!

"How was your day, baby?" Charles asked, trying to kiss her in the mouth, only catching her cheek when she deliberately turned her head.

"It was fine," she answered, brushing past him, putting a little more bounce in her ass as she headed for the bedroom, knowing he was watching.

Once she got to the room, she placed her purse on the dresser and sat on the edge of the bed to relieve her feet of her boots. It didn't take long for Charles to show up and stand in the doorway as though he was going to watch her undress.

"Should I run some bath water?" he asked.

"I'm taking a shower," she answered.

"Well, I'm about to start dinner," he told her. "Do you have any requests?"

"Nope."

Charles lingered a few seconds, then set out to start dinner. Ebony finished undressing, then headed for the bathroom. After turning on the shower, she stood under the shower head allowing the hot water to ease some of the tension in her body. As she started to lather her body with a soapy rag, there was a tap on the bathroom door.

"Sweetheart?" Charles entered.

"What, Charles?" she answered, rolling her eyes.

"You, um, need me to wash your back?"

Ebony already knew what he was up to. He hadn't seen, or touched her body in two days, and was using this as an initiative to do both. Being that she'd already been intentionally teasing him lately, she decided she would give him a chance to tease himself. Therefore, she deferred, handing him the rag and standing back on her legs, which is something most men found sexy, and, as she knew he would, Charles took his precious time. He started at her shoulders and seemed to do more caressing than washing, but Ebony didn't dare stop him or interrupt him as he mentally pleased himself. She just stood there like an obedient dog being groomed until he was done.

"Thank you, Charles!" she said as nice as she could, receiving the rag from him, noticing the bulge in his pants and lust in his eyes.

It boosted her ego to see the kind of effect she had on him, right now. He was at the point where he would give his right arm, just to touch her. Now, she was debating if she should give him some tonight, or snub him, so she could listen to him masturbate beside her again like he'd done last night when he thought she was asleep.

****

Girl, you a'ight?" Shonda asked after Sheila had undergone another coughing spell.

"I might have a cold," Sheila answered.

"Might, hell!" Shonda exclaimed, regarding her like she had a deadly disease that was highly contagious. "Your eyes are bloodshot red, and that same piece of snot has been hanging out your nose since briefing. You got the cooties!"

"Why you didn't tell me I had snot hanging out my nose!" Sheila exclaimed in a hushed tone, not to be heard by the inmates who were out of their cells.

"I just did."

"I can't believe you!" Shelia placed a hand over her nose. "You let me walk around with snot hanging out my nose?"

"I thought you knew," Shonda said, smiling. "Hell, I thought it was a fad."

"Stop playing!" Sheila punched her in the leg. "Do I really have—"

She went into another coughing spell, causing Shonda to roll her chair in the opposite direction.

"Girl, you should've stayed your infected ass at home!" Shonda said, laughing.

"Shut up!"

At that time, Lieutenant Baton, the shift supervisor for today, being that Mallery was off, showed up in the sally port. Sheila buzzed him in.

"Good morning, ladies!" he greeted, approaching the desk.

"Good morning!" they greeted him in unison as Sheila handed him the logbook.

"Um, Ms. Griffin might need the rest of the day off," Shonda told him.

"Why?" he asked, looking back and forth from the two.

"Look at her!" Shonda said. "Look at her eyes! You can't tell a sick person when you see one? It's a wonder she hasn't coughed up her lungs!"

"Yeah, she looks pretty sick to me," he stated, eyeing Sheila. "Ms. Griffin, do you need the rest of the day off?"

"I believe so," she answered, going into another spell.

"Well, let me find somebody to relieve you."

It took almost thirty minutes for her relieving officer to show up. Being that she didn't have any cold medications at home, Sheila made a stop at the nearest pharmacy and purchased cough syrup, cough drops, and Vicks Vapor Rub. Not willing to wait until she got home, she downed some cough syrup and popped a cough drop in the car before leaving the pharmacy.

By the time she made it home, the syrup had already started to take effect. She was hoping Andrew was out, job hunting, so she could get the proper rest that her body was in dire need of, but his car was in the same spot it was when she left that morning. She had already sensed he was lying about his job-hunting ventures. Now, it was confirmed. She was in her right mind to enter the apartment like a raging bull and let him have it, but her body, which was numb from the medication, wasn't up to it. Therefore, she decided, she would remit the task until after she was well rested. By then, he better have the world's greatest excuse for why he'd been lying about looking for a job, and why her apartment was still looking like a pigsty because she just knew he hadn't cleaned up.

But, upon entering the apartment, she saw that it was clean. In fact, the living room and kitchen looked as if she'd cleaned them herself. Seeing this, erased some of her anger. However, he still had some explaining to do.

By the looks of the place, it seemed as if Andrew had cleaned up and gone back to bed because it was extremely quiet. This elevated her anger because here it was almost twelve o'clock, and his lazy ass was still in bed.

Sheila was not going for this! Andrew was going to have to move out of her apartment, today! Better yet, she was about to wake him up right now and kick him out. The bedroom door was ajar, and Sheila was about to kick it open until she heard the sound of someone moaning like they were having sex. This caused her to stop in her tracks and listen. The moaning continued. Sheila didn't want to believe Andrew was actually having sex with another woman in her bed, but it didn't take a rocket scientist to confirm it. She knew she was going to have to face it. So, with tears welling up in her eyes, and butterflies in her stomach, she willed herself to kick the door open.

Andrew and Lieutenant Mallery, who were both naked and in the sixty-nine position, jolted out of the bed in opposite directions, putting the bed between them, and were now regarding her like deer caught in headlights.

"Oh, I'm 'bout to kill both of y'all asses!" Sheila yelled, then stormed off to the kitchen, where she slammed her purse down on the counter and rummaged through the silverware drawer for the biggest knife she could find.

****

When Shonda entered her house, she decided she would check on Sheila before taking a shower, but Sheila didn't answer the phone. Figuring she was probably resting, Shonda went on and took a thirty-something minute shower. Afterward, she climbed into bed and watched TV until she dozed off.

It seemed as if she had just closed her eyes when she was awakened by the musical ringtone of her cellular phone, but she couldn't have just fallen asleep, because she noticed it was now dark outside. The time on her screen right above Sheila's name and number showed 7:44 p.m.

"I called your sick ass earlier!" Shonda answered her phone. "How're you feeling?" All she could hear on the other end was sniffling, like Sheila was crying. "Sheila, what's wrong, boo-boo?"

"I caught Andrew cheating on me," she answered, breaking into a sob.

Shonda closed her eyes and took a deep breath. Now, she was extremely rabid, because ever since Sheila was harmed when they were young, Shonda had vowed to never let anyone else hurt her little cousin again and get away with it. So, yes, somebody had to pay the piper!

"Baby, do you need me to come over?"

"He brought that bitch in my house, Shonda!" Sheila hollered. "He had that bitch in my bed!"

"What bitch, baby?" Shonda asked, sensing that Sheila was familiar with *that bitch.*

She heard Sheila take a deep breath before answering. "Mallery."

"What!" Shonda's body seemed to automatically sit up. "I know you ain't talking about *that* Mallery!"

Sheila went on to explain how she'd caught them in the sixty-nine position, and how she had retrieved a knife from the kitchen, with the intent to cause them both harm, but was a little content to see them high-tailing it out of her apartment, half-naked. Then she cried herself to sleep.

"So, what're you gonna do?" Shonda asked.

"It's over!" Sheila answered. "I packed all of his stuff and sat it in the parking lot. He can't—"

"I'm talking about, Mallery," Shonda cut her off. "You'll have to see her at work. It's gonna be hard not to—"

"I'm not going back."

"You're not?"

"I'll start looking for another job, tomorrow," Sheila told her. "I'll call and tell them I'm resigning for personal reasons."

Shonda wanted to reason with her cousin, but she knew Sheila was thinking rationally, so she had no choice but to respect her decision.

"Do you need me to come over?" Shonda asked again.

"No, I'm good."

"Are you sure?"

"I'm positive."

"Alright," Shonda gave in. "If you feel like you need to talk, don't hesitate to call me."

Getting off the phone with Sheila, Shonda got out of bed and headed for the kitchen to see if she could force herself to eat something, being that she was beyond hungry. She managed to consume two, microwaved chicken sandwiches while mulling over everything Sheila had told her.

The last time Sheila had been heart-broken by a man which was a few days before they'd met the Kingz. Shonda had caught up with the guy, punched one of his teeth out, and slapped his new girlfriend, who looked as though she wanted to say something. Neither one of them defied to oppose her. Now, once again, she felt she had to avenge her cousin's distress.

Shonda watched TV until she'd fallen asleep, this time awakened by her alarm clock. She was so anxious to get to work and confront Lieutenant Mallery, she got dressed in record-breaking time. She was surprised to see that she was the third officer in the briefing room when the room was usually packed whenever she'd arrived, but she waited patiently on the back row as the other officers slowly piled in, taking their seats.

Once the room had gotten packed, Shonda was beginning to wonder if Mallery was even going to show up, but the second she'd thought it, Mallery strutted into the room and up to the podium with the roll call roster in hand. As always, she went right into roll call and post assignments. Shonda couldn't believe the bitch had the audacity to carry on like she hadn't violated her cousin. Then, when she called Sheila's name and didn't get a reply, she smiled to herself and continued. After Mallery's brief and a few questions from some of the staff members. Shonda was the first one to leave the room. She stood outside the door, while the others hustled for the elevators.

The sound of Mallery's shrill laughter reached Shonda before Mallery did, which added fuel to the fire that was already big enough to consume half of the planet. Seconds later, Mallery and another female emerged from the room. Seeing Shonda, Mallery stopped in her tracks, apprehension in her eyes. But it was a little too late for that.

Shonda put all her strength into that first swing, punching Mallery in the mouth, bursting her bottom lip on contact, but she couldn't let up that easy. She followed up with a hail of blows, in which Mallery tried her best to block. Shonda felt someone grab her shoulder. Thinking it was the officer Mallery was just talking to, she turned and swung, punching the intruder square in the nose, causing instant drainage of blood.

When Shonda attacked Lieutenant Mallery, she knew she'd lost her job, but when she turned and struck the Captain, she knew she'd lost her freedom.

CHAPTER 10

Sheila left her apartment around ten, in search of new employment. Being that she didn't want to go back to fast foods, she avoided the restaurants, filling out applications at South Dekalb Mall, North Dekalb Mall, Toys-R-Us, and two banks. She still ended up filling out applications at three fast-food restaurants, just in case she needed something to fall back on until something better comes up.

She had called the jail before leaving her apartment, to tell the supervisor that she was resigning, due to personal issues, but was informed that the supervisor couldn't come to the phone because they had a situation. Instead of leaving a message with the active supervisor, Sheila vowed to call back later.

It was after two o'clock when she returned home. Being that she was a bit exhausted and still heart-broken, she decided to take a nap. As soon as she laid down, her cell phone rang. The number on the screen belonged to her grandmother, who'd raised her and Shonda after both of their mothers were killed in a car crash when they were kids, while on their way home from work.

"Hey, Nanna!" Sheila answered, sounding more ecstatic than she felt.

"Hey, baby!" her grandmother replied. "Ya sistah done went and got locked up."

"Shonda?" Sheila asked, being that their grandmother had always referred to them as sisters.

"What other sistah you got, child?"

"Sheila?" Shonda's voice came through the phone.

"Girl, what've you done?" Sheila asked, almost feeling as though she knew the answer.

When Shonda gave her the summary of what happened, Sheila realized she was the *situation* the active supervisor had mentioned when she called earlier.

"So, what did they charge you with?" Sheila asked, feeling like it was all her fault.

"Two counts of simple assault," Shonda answered. "No bond."

"You should go to court, tomorrow, right?"

"I should."

"When you get a bond, will you be able to pay it?" Their grand-mother intervened.

"Yes, ma'am," answered Shonda.

Although Shonda sounded quite certain, Sheila knew she was lying to keep their grandmother from offering what little money she had saved up, knowing she would give her left leg for her grand-babies, which was something they would never impose on her, if they could help it.

After getting off the phone with them, Sheila called Ebony and informed her on Shonda's situation.

"That's why I didn't tell Erica about my situation with Charles," said Ebony, who was doing someone's hair at the moment.

"I didn't think Shonda would pull this stunt," Sheila asserted. "Then she did it at the jail."

"I just hope the bond ain't high," Ebony said. "Cause my money is looking a lil funny, also, but I'll give what I can for my girl."

"This is crazy!" said Sheila, slowing shaking her head.

"I know," Ebony agreed. "Let me finish this client. I'll call you when I get home."

"Okay."

Sheila ended the call, then headed for the kitchen to pour herself a glass of orange juice, but before she could find something to drink out of, someone knocked on her front door. She found it odd, be-cause she didn't have company unless it was Shonda or Ebony, and she knew exactly where they were at this moment.

Her only guess now was Andrew, and this pissed her off be-cause he had no business knocking on her door. She had tossed all of his belongings out, so there was nothing left for him to come back for, but instead of ignoring him, she headed for the door, figuring this was her chance to give him a piece of her mind. When she peered through the peephole, she was not looking at Andrew, and just when she thought her day was going to get worse, God had other plans for her. Tears of joy welled up in her eyes as she fumbled with the locks and snatched the door open.

"What's up, G.I. Jane!" Sheila exclaimed, throwing her arms around her friend, who she had not seen in six months.

Theresa, who was clad in full Army fatigue, hat and carrying a large duffle bag, embraced her friend back. "I missed you too, heifer!" she joked. "Where's that super sexy boyfriend you talked about in your letter?"

"Are you gonna stand out there in the cold?" Sheila asked, ready to go ahead and hand Theresa the bad news about Andrew and Shonda, to get it out of the way. "Give me this."

Sheila grabbed the duffle bag from Theresa, took it to the guest room, then returned to the living room, where Theresa had taken off her coat and hat and was seated on the sofa.

"I don't even know where to begin," Sheila said, joining her friend on the sofa.

"Don't tell me y'all broke up already!"

Sheila took a deep breath, then told Theresa how she'd caught Andrew with Mallery, to how Shonda had taken it upon herself to seek retribution, which landed her in jail.

"Damn!" Theresa replied, after hearing the news. "So, all of this happened within twenty-four hours? Shonda just got locked up, this morning?"

"Yeah."

"To be honest, I don't know what I would've done had I walked in on some shit like that," Theresa admitted. "I probably would've stabbed both of their asses! What's going on with, Ebony?"

"You wanna go by her shop and surprise her?" Sheila asked, feeling she should let Ebony tell of her own affairs.

"Yeah, let's do that," answered Theresa. "I'm anxious to see the shop."

They donned their coats and left the apartment, headed for Gwinnett County.

"Glamor Girlz," Theresa read the shop's sign as Sheila pulled into the plaza and found a parking spot. "She has White customers too, huh?"

"White, Asian, Spanish," Sheila answered, cutting the engine. "Ya girl got it going on!"

They dismounted and headed for the shop. Sheila couldn't wait to see Ebony's face light up when she saw Theresa, but upon entering the salon, they saw that Ebony's station was empty, which made Sheila look back out at the parking lot for Ebony's car. The car was there.

"Did Ebony leave?" Sheila asked no one in particular.

Before anyone could answer, Ebony, emerged from the restroom and with her head down, brushing something off her shirt. When she finally looked up, her eyes widened with surprise, which accommodated the broad smile on her face.

"Heeey!" Ebony exclaimed, approaching Theresa with her arms wide open. "Welcome back!"

Ebony did the honors of introducing Theresa to the rest of the stylists and insisted on taking her and Sylvia to dinner. Once Ebony had cleaned her station and gathered her things, the three of them exited the salon and climbed into Ebony's car.

"Y'all had just missed, Erica," Ebony told them as she started the car and pulled out of the lot.

"How is she holding up?" Theresa, who was seated beside Ebony, inquired.

"She's doing better than I thought she would. How are *you* holding up?"

"I'm suspended in the air, right now," she answered. "I'll be okay, once I get my feet on solid ground."

"Where are you staying?"

"Nowhere at the moment."

"Girl, you know you can stay with me," Sheila intervened, knowing Theresa didn't have a place to stay, because the guy she was staying with before she left for the Army, ended up moving away with another woman. Plus, she was not on good terms with her family back in Dallas, Texas.

"What about money?" Ebony asked. "I already know you can't fit mine or Sheila's clothes. So, you'll need some new stuff."

"Yeah, I definitely need some new attire."

"You okay back there, Sheila?" Ebony asked.

"Huh? Yeah, I'm okay," Sheila answered, realizing she had been thinking about Andrew.

She was really missing him.

****

It was Saturday, Sheila and Theresa had spent the past two days job hunting. Now, they were at the Cumberland Mall, shopping for clothes for Theresa, being that Ebony had given her five hundred dollars.

"I think those tacos are working on me," Sheila said rubbing her stomach as she watched Theresa pick out jeans.

That's why they build public restrooms," Theresa replied, smiling to herself.

"They didn't build 'em for *me!*" Sheila protested. "I'll go behind some bushes before I sit on one of those crab-infested toilets! They ain't gon' have the skin on *my* booty breaking out!"

Theresa was laughing hysterically now. She already knew Sheila was going to come off like that, and she hadn't laughed like that since the last time she was around her girls. Now, the only person she hadn't reunited with yet, was Shonda. She went to court, Thursday, and received a two-hundred-thousand-dollar bond, in which twelve percent of that would have to be paid, in order for her to make bail.

They would be lucky to scrape up two percent of that.

"Girl, you crazy!" Theresa exclaimed, after getting her laughter under control. "Let me pick out a few more pairs of pants, then we can head out."

Once Theresa had chosen her pants and paid for everything, they left the boutique. As they neared the exit of the mall, some guy called Sheila's name, causing them both to turn around. The guy, approaching who was accompanied by two other men, was Tino, Shonda's high school sweetheart. They were still dating, when Theresa moved to Georgia, in 2000. She still didn't know how they'd broken up.

"What's going on ladies?" Tino approached.

"Hey, Tino," they spoke in unison, with Sheila asking if he'd moved back to Georgia, being that he'd moved to California.

"Nah," he answered. "I'm just down here on business. Where's the rest of, Destiny's Child?"

Sheila giggled. "Ebony is running her salon and Shonda is in jail."

"*Jail!*" he let out. "Who she done beat up?"

Sheila gave him a brief run-down of what happened, making sure to include how much her bond was.

"Ain't nobody gon' pay it?" he asked.

Theresa answered, "Ain't nobody got that kind of money!"

"I thought the home team had left y'all straight."

"Apparently not," Sheila replied, knowing he was referring to The Kingz. "We'll find a way to get her out."

"That's what's up. Tell her to get at me when she gets out."

****

Sitting in a cell of the medical ward, all day was driving Shonda crazy. She was already feeling as though she was incompetent to stand trial. She respected the jail's policy of housing her on the medical floor for her safety, being that she was a detention officer, but she would rather take her chances in the general population.

Shonda was allowed an hour out of her cell, every day, but only used that time to shower, walk around and chat with some of the patients, or officers, who were only being nosey, trying to find out why she'd assaulted Lieutenant Mallery and Captain Shaw.

It didn't matter, because she was doing whatever she could to not allow her boredom to force her to the phone. The last time she'd used the phone, was Thursday to let Sheila and her grandmother know that she'd been to court and received a bond. When Sheila put Theresa on the phone, it made her happy that her friend had made it back in one piece, but sad, because she wasn't there to welcome her home, and couldn't celebrate the fact that her friend had endeavored to become successful.

Shonda thought about working out, but it wouldn't do her any good, being that she didn't have enough food on her stomach. She would only pick over the food they served. She had money on her when she was arrested, but wouldn't be able to make commissary, until next week.

Right now, her stomach was hurting from hunger, so being that it was already a little after 10:00 p.m., she decided to lay down and force herself to sleep. It took almost an hour, but she had succeeded, only to be awakened, moments later, by a female detention officer, telling her that she'd made bond.

Shonda could not believe this! She didn't know a soul who possessed twenty-two thousand dollars, but that didn't stop her from packing her things like the officer told her to. Once she was dressed out in some old, mildew-smelling clothes they'd found for her, she had to sit in intake for another four hours before she was able to sign herself out, but she had already placed a call to Sheila, via the pay phone, which is why she and Theresa were waiting in the lobby for her when she was released.

"Hey, y'all!" Shonda hugged her girls feeling like she'd done a bid.

"Girl, you smell like old folks!" Sheila joked. "Whose great-granddaddy you borrowed those clothes from?"

"They gave me these."

"You still don't know who paid your bond?" Theresa asked.

"Nah," she answered. "As a matter of fact, Sheila, you gotta take me to the bonding company to fill out some paperwork."

When they got to the bonding company, Shonda didn't have to wonder any longer who'd paid her bond, because his government name to her surprise was on the paperwork.

Playa Ray

CHAPTER 11

Getting her car out of impound had put another dent in Shonda's account, which she could not afford, but she needed her ride. She also needed another job, which is why she had been out all week seeking employment. Sheila had managed to get hired at the Cumberland Mall, as a security guard, which she would start the following week. Theresa had gotten a job at Wal-Mart, through a temp agency. Shonda knew she was treading on thin ice by applying for jobs that were known for doing background checks, being that she had those fresh charges, but she really needed a job.

Now, it was Thursday, and Shonda had just pulled into her driveway. She checked the mailbox before entering the house, where she stood at the kitchen counter looking over her bills, which reminded her that she had to call the bank to check her balance. When she was told that she only had a little over eight hundred dollars, she knew she had to do what she had been thinking about, ever since her release, sell the house.

"Why don't you sell the car instead?" Ebony asked over the phone after Shonda explained the only option she'd come up with.

"Because, I can get more for the house," she explained. "Plus, I can do a lot more with that money."

"So, how much would you sell it for?"

"No less than fifty thousand, I guess," Shonda answered. "I'll move back into an apartment, get a job, and go from there."

"Ebony, won't Charles buy the house?" Sheila, who was also on the line, asked.

"He should," answered Ebony. "I mean that's what he does."

"So, you could easily make that arrangement," Sheila insisted.

"Maybe, first, I have to know if Shonda is serious about selling her house."

"I don't have a choice, right now," Shonda asserted. "The sooner, the better."

"No less than fifty?"

"Sixty-five," Shonda quickly changed her mind, considering she'd paid eighty-five for it. "That's the lowest I'll go."

****

After getting off the phone with her friends, Ebony went on to prepare dinner and her spiel for Charles, who was now taking a bath in the water she'd run for him. Now, she was feeling it was a good thing she'd run the water. It could work in her favor when she delivered her line to him about buying Shonda's house. If she gets the feeling, he's going to decline for the fact that he doesn't agree with her friends, then she was going to resort to Plan B, *seduction.*

She had already broken her rendezvous' down to three times a week, so, being that they were not due to have intercourse until tomorrow, he would be more than happy to see things her way.

"So, how's the remodeling going on that house in Clayton?" Ebony asked over dinner, which was one of her warm-up questions.

"They finished that up, yesterday," Charles answered, dabbing at his mouth with a napkin. "Tomorrow, I meet up with the couple who'll be renting it."

"Have you found another house for sale yet?"

"Not yet."

"I know where one is."

"Where?"

"In Decatur."

"Did you see the price?"

"They want seventy," Ebony told him, hoping to get her friend five thousand more than the lowest she would accept.

"Did you get a number?"

"I'll give it to you later," she said, trying to prolong revealing Shonda's identity.

After dinner, Ebony tended to the dishes. When she was done, she entered the bedroom, where Charles was already in bed, watching TV. This was when she decided she would go ahead and initiate Plan B, anyway. So, with her back to him, she began to slowly undress. Once she was down to her panties and bra, she made like she was getting something from the bottom drawer of the dresser, bending all the way over, knowing she had his undivided attention.

After tying her hair into a wrap, she climbed into bed, under the covers. Out of the corner of her eyes, she caught Charles watching her, but made no indication of it as she pretended to be interested in the television, but all the while, she was wondering if she'd given him an erection. She glanced over to see if she could spot a rise under the bedspreads, but the only rise she was able to see was from his bulging stomach.

Being that Ebony was both, curious about his erection and ready to get this over with, she reached over and grabbed his crotch through his boxers. Yes, he was fully erected! It would be a lie for Ebony to deny that this didn't turn her on. As she slowly caressed his manhood, she moved closer to him and began kissing on his neck. When she moved her mouth up to his ear and began kissing, licking and nibbling on it, Charles closed his eyes and moaned.

"Take your boxers off," she whispered in his ear.

Charles didn't hesitate, but he didn't move like he was in a rush to get the treat, she had for him. Once he'd tossed his boxers on the floor, Ebony folded the covers back and went down on him, sucking the tip, then periodically forcing him as far as he could reach past her tonsil.

Charles was moaning like a savage beast now, but Ebony knew she couldn't keep at this because Charles had a tendency of reaching his climax quicker than the average man. So, once she felt he was at that point, she stopped. Then, taking off her panties, she stood over him with her back to him, squatted down and used her hand to guide him inside her. Being that Charles was always thrilled about having her from the back, it didn't take long for him to explode inside of her.

Ebony didn't get hers, but it was okay because as soon as he fell asleep, she was going to take her vibrator into the main bathroom and make it do what it do. For now, she dismounted and headed for the main bathroom to wash up. When she'd returned, Charles was in their bathroom. She took this time to write down Shonda's name and number and placed it on the nightstand on his side of the bed. Then, putting her panties back on, she climbed back into bed, just as Charles emerged from the bathroom.

"That information is on your nightstand," she told him, once he'd climbed in beside her.

She had her back to him, but by the movement of the bed, she could tell he was going for the number.

"Shonda?" he asked. *"Your friend?"*

****

It was Monday, and the weekend was finally over. Shonda felt as though this was her lucky day. She didn't know what kind of persuasion Ebony had used on Charles, but he had called her Friday and claimed he would be more than happy to come by today and check out the house, which is why she'd gotten up early and conducted an overhaul of the place. Everything seemed to be in exceptional condition. Now it was fifteen minutes until eleven, and Shonda, clad in a tan business suit and heels, was wiping down the oakwood cabinets in the kitchen when the doorbell rang. She made sure to do a once-over before heading for the door, where she peered through the curtain to see Charles standing on the porch, in a gray suit.

"Good morning!" he greeted when she'd opened the door.

"Good morning!" she returned. "Come on in." Once he entered, she locked the door back. "So, where do you wanna start?"

"I guess we'll start here, impress me."

Shonda took that as her cue and led the way. Charles didn't say a word as she gave him a tour of the house. Once they'd cleared every room, they exited the back door, circled the house and re-entered the back door.

"And your asking price is seventy?" Charles asked once they were back in the living room.

"It is," Shonda answered, trying to recall when she'd said anything to him about an asking price.

"I'll give you sixty," he told her.

Being that Shonda knew all about bargaining strategies, she didn't take offense to his approach. Considering she really needed the money, she decided to play the game like it was supposed to be played.

"Sixty-eight is a reasonable price for a house in such a good condition as this one. Unless you feel otherwise."

"I don't," he admitted. "But sixty-five is my final offer."

Yes, today was, indeed, her lucky day. Once they'd done the necessary paperwork and he granted her a week to move, Charles left, and Shonda made the phone call she'd been meaning to make since the day she'd bonded out.

"Yeah, what up?" Tino answered.

"Are you busy?" Shonda asked.

"If I was busy, I wouldn't have answered the phone," he replied. "It took you forever to hit me up."

"I had to get some things situated," Shonda explained. "I just sold my house today. I'm about to take this check to the bank. Once it clears, I'll be able to pay your money back."

"I didn't ask you to pay me back."

Shonda knew better. "I appreciate it, but I'm paying the money back."

"Okay," he gave in. "So, where will you be staying?"

Shonda answered, "I have a week to move. If I haven't found an apartment by then, I guess I'll be at Sheila's."

"That's what's up," Tino asserted. "So, I guess I'll be hearing from you again, huh?"

"As soon as this check clears."

Tino hesitated a few seconds before saying, "You know I got you if you're trying to get all the way right. I got that ex-girlfriend discount waiting for you."

"I'm good, Tino," Shonda proclaimed, in disbelief that he would come at her like that.

But he didn't let up. "Well, if things get rough and you feel like you need to make a move, make sure it's in my direction. I got you."

"I'll remember that, Tino."

Shonda hung up and tried to figure out why Tino had stepped to her like that? Like she would be interested in buying weight from him or anybody else. It's not like she wouldn't know what to do with the product, because she did. It's just that time wasn't that hard on her to the point where she would have to resort to that.

Now having nothing to do, Shonda decided to go ahead and get a jump on her packing. She went out and bought cardboard boxes and scotch tape. After depositing the check into her account, she ate lunch, then returned home to pack. While she was packing, she received a call from Theresa, telling her that she wasn't having any luck with finding a full-time job, which gave Shonda an idea.

"I got a job for you, right now," Shonda told her.

"What's that?"

"Help me pack," Shonda answered. "I'll pay you seven hundred, but you'll have to wait until the check clears."

"You sold the house?"

"Hell yeah! I got a week to move out. I'm just getting a head start. Do I have to pick you up?'

"Nah," answered Theresa. "I got Sheila's half-of-car. I have to pick her up around nine-fifteen."

"Shoot, that's enough time!"

"I'm already en route."

Shonda didn't need the help, but she knew her friend needed the money. Plus, it would be good to have Theresa's company, right about now. Maybe they could reminisce about the past. She was about to take a break until Theresa showed, but since she'd already begun packing her shoes into a box, she decided to finish that task.

After neatly stacking her shoes into the cardboard boxes, Shonda saw that she had enough room for a few more things. As she looked atop the shelf, she spotted the cylinder tin can she'd had for over four years. What once held cheese flavored popcorn, was now storage for miscellaneous items, such as various hair combs, brushes, large earrings, and pieces of broken jewelry, which didn't take up much of the container.

Although the diameter of the can surpass those of her shoeboxes, Shonda knew it would fit inside the large box. However, when she reached and pulled it down, she noticed it was heavier than it was the last time she'd held it, which was highly unusual. As she held the container in the crook of her arm, Shonda pulled the top off and gasped at the sight of the brick shaped item wrapped in aluminum foil.

Playa Ray

CHAPTER 12

The week had gone by pretty fast. It was Friday, and Shonda was all packed and ready to move, although she had two more days left in the house. She'd managed to rent a storage bin for her belongings and put in applications for an apartment at three different locations.

Now, she was supervising the three movers as they moved her furniture to the moving truck. Once all the furniture was out, they began moving the boxes, and Shonda could not pry her eyes off the box she had marked, *Shoes.*

She still hadn't told anyone she'd found a kilo of uncooked cocaine in her closet. It didn't take long for her to figure out who'd left it there. She was still thinking she should drive to East Lake and bring it to Trent's attention, with hopes of getting Mario out of the jam he was in or hold on to it until Mario contacted her.

That's if he's still alive.

Shonda had followed the movers to the storage yard. Once everything was stored, she applied the security lock she'd bought, then headed for Sheila's apartment with the rest of her belongings. When she arrived, she used the spare key Sheila gave her to let herself in. Once she'd stored her things in the bedroom Theresa was staying in, she reposed on the small bed and used her cell phone to check on her apartment. The landlord of Allen Temple Apartments informed her that her application was accepted and that she could come by Monday and pay the deposit fee.

Shonda was overwhelmed by the news. The check had not yet cleared, but she had enough to pay the fee and possibly get her things moved in on that same day. Now, her mind reverted back to the kilo of cocaine. She was hoping like hell nothing happened at the storage yard that would prompt authorities to do a thorough search of everyone's storage bin because her ass was definitely going back to jail.

Shonda didn't know she'd fallen asleep until she was awakened by the clattering sound of dishes and the aroma of food being cooked. She looked around the room and noticed the door had been closed. Then, she spotted Theresa's work uniform lying across the chair and realized Theresa was the one who'd closed it.

"Look who's awakened from the dead!" said Sheila, when Shonda entered the kitchen.

"Girl, you sleep too hard!" said Theresa, who was seated on one of the two stools at the counter while Sheila cooked.

"I heard your big feet ass!" Shonda replied.

"Oh, I know you ain't talking about nobody's feet!" Theresa came back. "Not with those talons hanging off the end of your shit!"

"Damn!" Sheila exclaimed, laughing along with them.

"What's for dinner?" Shonda asked, after containing her laughter.

"Hamburger Helper," Sheila answered.

"That's what's up!" Shonda said, taking a seat on the stool beside Theresa. "Y'all, we need to go out tonight. All four of us."

"Girl, it's pouring down out there!" Sheila told her.

"It's not raining inside the club," Shonda said.

She really wanted to get her girls together and just go out and have fun.

"It may not be raining inside the club," said Theresa. "But we ain't got no club money, right now. Me and Sheila just started working."

"Well, we need to find *something* to do!"

"I got some cards," said Sheila. "If one of y'all would drive to the store and get some Moscato, we can drink, play cards, listen to some music and talk about these trifling ass men."

They had all agreed to Sheila's plan, so, after dinner, Theresa and Shonda went out for the Moscato, while Sheila set out chips and dip. Now, the three of them were seated around the coffee table, on the sofa's cushions, playing poker as they enjoyed the alcohol, chips, and music coming from the stereo.

"It's too bad, Ebony, ain't here," said Theresa. "It just don't feel right without the whole wreckin' crew."

"She would've shown up," Sheila said. "She just didn't wanna take a chance on the road with that rain coming down like that."

"Now, she's stuck at home with her husband to be, playing wife to be," Shonda summarized with a smirk.

Theresa asserted, "That's a good thing!"

"Why is that?" asked Shonda.

"Because," Theresa answered, taking a sip of her drink. "This is that good lovemaking weather."

"And speaking of lovemaking," Shonda started, smiling. "You ain't had no dick since you've been back."

"Dick is the last thing on my mind, right now.'

Sheila furrowed her eyebrows at the statement. "Say what?"

"Dick is the last thing on my mind, right now," Theresa repeated.

"You didn't happen to drop the soap while you were in training, did you?" Sheila joked, causing Theresa and Shonda to laugh.

"Right now, I'm more concerned about getting my paper right," Theresa admitted. "I need my own place and car. If a nigga ain't gonna help me with those, then he can keep his worthless ass dick!"

"I'll toast to that!" said Sheila, holding her plastic cup up and making the toast with the girls. "I'm tired of being broke, living from check to check, and dealing with these nothing ass dudes! It's about time we start screaming *M-O-B, Money Over Busters!*"

"Yeah!" Theresa agreed. "We're some topnotch looking bitches! Ain't no way in hell we should be living like this! We should be living in big houses and driving expensive cars!"

"Business owners!" Sheila chimed in.

Listening to them rant on like this, made Shonda think about the kilo. It wasn't hers, but, at the same time, it was. Mario had taken her through a lot of changes and caused her a lot of money. So, in actuality, the key, indeed, belonged to her, fuck Mario!

Being that James had taught her the essence of the drug game, she knew she could take the key and multiply it by whatever number she so chose. This could really be the break she and her girls needed, wanted and deserved, but first, she had to know if they are willing to cross the threshold of a dangerous, and male-dominated game.

****

Monday was finally here. Shonda had a lot to accomplish today, so she got up early, showered, cooked breakfast for her, Sheila and Theresa who both had to be to work at ten, then made her exit, shortly after they did.

Shonda's first destination was Allen Temple Apartments in Atlanta, for her final interview with the landlord, and to fill out the necessary paperwork. She paid the deposit fee for her three-bedroom apartment, then left with the intent to get her things moved in, ASAP. First, she had to call the bank to see if the check had cleared. When she was informed that it had, her plans changed. While still sitting in Allen Temple's parking lot, she dialed Tino's number.

"What's crackin'?" he answered.

"The check cleared," she told him. "I need your routing and account numbers."

After giving her the information, he asked, "So what're you gonna do about a lawyer?"

"I don't know yet. You know one?"

"The one I had for that assault charge."

Shonda remembered the assault charge Tino caught when he'd shot two guys in front of her and several other people. Despite the witnesses that testified against him in court, his lawyer managed to get him off with probation, community service and a fine. Considering this she obtained the lawyer's number from, Tino.

"Should I mention you?" she asked.

"You shouldn't have to," Tino answered. "He may charge you an arm and leg, but he's worth it. If you can't cover the whole cost, let me know. I still got that ex-girlfriend discount on them thangs for you."

"Bye, Tino!"

Shonda concluded the call, smiling to herself. She did kinda miss Tino. His sex drive was just way too high for her. Dismissing the thought, she drove out of the parking lot and headed for the bank, where she was going to make the transaction for Tino and write fifteen hundred-dollar checks for Sheila, Theresa, Ebony, and Erica.

****

"Is Pam in?"

Ebony looked up from her customer's hair she was braiding, to see one of Pam's customers giving her an expecting look. This really pissed Ebony off, because Pam had the audacity to call in, pretending to be sick, but didn't have the decency to call and notify her scheduled clients.

"No," Ebony answered as calmly as she could. "She called in sick. You can reschedule with her, or see if one of the other girls could fit you in.

"You must be full?"

"I have two more clients," Ebony told her. "They should tie me over until closing time, or close to it."

"I'll just reschedule," the client said, then exited the shop.

Seconds later, Erica approached, clad in her Baby Phat shirt, jeans and boots, which seemed to be the only clothing brand Erica had been sporting for the past two weeks. Whoever her *friend* was, he was spending a lot of money on her, considering the jewelry, also, but for some reason, she would not tell Ebony who he is.

"I got Meagan shampooed and under the dryer," Erica informed. "Once I do this relaxer for Khandi, I'll be ready to take up the lunch list. You already know what you want?"

"Not really," Ebony answered. "I really don't have an appetite."

"What's wrong?"

"I guess it's just one of those days. I got plenty of rest last night, but I still feel tired. As a matter of fact, put me down for a salad."

"What kind?"

Before Ebony could answer, the entrance bell sounded, indicating someone had entered. They both looked to see Shonda, who had a broad smile plastered on her face.

"Hey, Glamor Girlz!" Shonda greeted everyone.

"Looks like somebody got some last night!" Erica asserted, prompting laughter from everyone.

"I plead the fifth!" Shonda said, throwing her hands up in mock surrender. "I will not be the topic of y'all next gossip column! Y'all be getting *too* explicit!"

"So, what brings you by on a rain-threatening day like this?" Ebony asked.

"To see my girls," she answered, pulling out the two checks she'd written for them handing them both to Erica, being that Ebony's hands were soiled with hair products. "And to give y'all these."

"Damn!" Erica exclaimed, looking at the content of the checks. "I guess I can put you on my BFF list now."

"Let me see!" said Ebony. Once Erica showed them to her, she said, "Shonda, you didn't have to do that for me, I'm good."

"Girl, it ain't nothing but money," Shonda asserted. "I hate to be in and out, but I have other things to do."

"That's okay," said Ebony. "Thanks for the check."

Erica hugged Shonda. "Yeah, thank you, girl."

"Y'all more than welcome," Shonda replied, hugged Ebony, then made her exit.

The rest of the day breezed by. It was almost four o'clock when Ebony finished her last client. Being that she was still tired and ready to go home, she delegated the lock-up chore to Khandi and Erica, then headed out. When she'd made it home, she wasn't surprised to see that Charles had not made it in yet. This was good because she didn't feel like being bothered.

She just wanted to kick her shoes off and jump right in the bed, with the intent to shower later, and Ebony did just that. For some reason, she could not bring herself to fall asleep, which was why she was still awake when Charles got in. Still not up to being bothered, she pretended to be sleeping, but she listened as he quietly, but hastily moved around the room for a good minute or two before leaving back out. Moments later, she heard the sound of the shower. She figured she could will herself to sleep before he was done, but as she tried to think of something that would help her doze, she was hit with déjà vu.

Ebony didn't just want to jump to conclusions. Just because Charles had rushed off to take a shower, didn't necessarily mean he was guilty of anything. Besides, if he was still messing around on her, he had been doing a good job at hiding it. So, dismissing the thought, she continued with her struggle to fall asleep— and succeeded.

When Ebony had awakened, she saw that it was dark outside, and there was no sign of Charles. The room was dark, but she had no problem finding the door that Charles had closed. Exiting the bedroom, she moved along the quiet house until she came upon the living room, where Charles was seated on the sofa, talking on his cellular, with the TV turned down.

"Do you want me to cook?" he asked, noticing her.

"You can," she answered. "I'm about to take a shower."

Ebony returned to the bedroom, gathered her bath accessories, and headed for the main bathroom. As soon as she entered and closed the door, her eyes automatically locked onto the dirty clothes hamper. Once again, she was hit with déjà vu, and the urge to probe the hamper was extremely high. Therefore, she placed her things on the shelf, then lifted the top. Wasting no time, she grabbed his balled-up shirt. She was about to pick up his boxers until her nose caught a whiff of a particular scent coming off his shirt. Disregarding the boxers, she put the shirt up to her nose and inhaled the fragrance.

The perfume was blended with Charles' cologne but overpowered it. Ebony already knew it wasn't something she wore, and she couldn't call out the name of the fragrance to save her life, but she was sure she'd encountered it, several times. Possibly worn by someone she dealt with on a regular.

Playa Ray

CHAPTER 13

"Maybe she changed her mind."

Shonda looked across the table at Sheila, who'd made the comment. It was Friday, and the girls had all decided to meet at Jack's Bar and Grill, in Buckhead. Being that Shonda was the one that instigated the outing, she was hoping like hell Ebony showed up because she really needed to have a heart to heart with her girls about something that had been on her mind for a while.

She still had not found employment, but, this week, she had managed to move into her new apartment, and pay the lawyer's retainer's fee, which was five thousand of the twenty-five thousand he was charging her to take her case.

"Sorry I'm late, heifers!" Ebony approached the table, taking off her coat, then took a seat beside Sheila.

"It's better late than never," said Theresa, who was seated beside Shonda. "How was your Thanksgiving?"

"Well," Ebony started. "I was thankful that Charles spent it with his family, and I spent it with mine!"

"Now, you can have a stress free outing wit 'cha girls," Shonda said, trying to take Ebony's mind off of Charles' infidelity because she was going to need Ebony's undivided attention when she conveyed her thoughts to them. "As a matter of fact, you need something to drink, something relaxing."

Shonda flagged down one of the waiters and ordered a bottle of Patron. As they drank and conversated Shonda noted everyone's demeanor. She saw how the alcohol had put them all in a more relaxed mood, especially Ebony.

"I wanna make a toast," Shonda said, in mid-conversation.

"Sheila asked, "To what?"

"Not to *what— to who*," Shonda rejoined.

"Well, who do you wanna make a toast to?"

"To, The Queenz," Shonda stated, ready to spring her pitch.

"And who are, The Queenz?" asked Ebony.

"We are."

"I can't tell!" Ebony contended.

"For real!" Theresa chimed in. "We may *look* like queens, but we damn sho' don't *live* like queens!"

"But that doesn't mean that we *can't* live like queens," Shonda challenged.

"It sounds like you know something we don't," Theresa expressed, taking a sip of her drink. "Do tell."

Shonda took a sip of her drink, then eyed each one of them before telling them about the kilo that Mario had hidden in her closet the day, he'd stolen her car. Then, she went on to tell them about what James had taught her about the preparation and distribution of the product.

"This may seem farfetched," Shonda continued. "But we can do the same thing The Kingz did."

"Girl, you done lost your damn mind!" exclaimed Sheila. "That's gotta be the alcohol talking, cause ain't no way in hell. You really believe we're going to attempt a dangerous stunt like that? I don't know how you can see us standing on the corner doing that, because I can't!"

"We won't be standing on the corner," Shonda assured her. "We'll be selling weight. That's the advantage that we'll have, starting off with a key. Once we make the right contacts and build a clientele, we can begin expanding our product and our region."

"You're right," Ebony said. "That does sound farfetched. Besides, we're women, that's a man's game."

"It's *anybody's* game," Shonda argued. "A strong-minded man ain't no different from a strong-minded woman. It's about knowing what you want and stopping at nothing to get it. Are y'all with me, or not?"

****

It was almost twelve o'clock when Shonda returned to her apartment. At first, she had wanted to hang out at a club, but after having that conversation with her girls, now, all she wanted to do was shower and relax. The shower had gone well, but relaxation seemed to be impossible. It seemed as though she couldn't keep her eyes closed long enough to allow herself to doze off. All she could think about was how her girls had declined something that she knew would change their lives, completely, and put them at the financial level that they deserve to be at.

Shonda was angry, but she couldn't be mad at them for being precarious about something they had never experienced like she had when she was with James. They knew that the drug game was dangerous. Shonda knew the drug game was dangerous. However, for some reason, her determination seemed to outweigh her fear, which was why, now, she got out of bed, cut on the light, and headed for the closet.

After removing the kilo from the tin can, she laid the package on the bed and stared at it. She knew what she needed but didn't know where to obtain the two main implements that would avail her in the first phase of preparation. But she knew who could point her in the right direction.

Shonda had no idea as to what time it was in California, but she called Tino, anyway.

"Talk to me," Tino answered, shortly.

"What 'cha doing?" she asked, trying to detect his mood before going into her purpose for calling.

"I'm chillin' with one of my female friends," he told her. "What's up?"

"Is your phone safe?"

"Talk."

"I need a glass pot and scale."

"I'll holla back," he said, quickly disconnecting.

Shonda was finally able to get some sleep, knowing that she now had one ally. She didn't hear from Tino until Monday afternoon, while she was checking her mailbox.

"I'm here," she answered her cellular.

"First date, two o'clock."

It didn't take long for Shonda to discern what Tino was telling her, which was why, at 1:40, she was pulling into the Underground Atlanta's parking garage, where Theresa was occupying the toll booth with another female employee.

"Hey girl!" Theresa greeted. "What're you up to?"

"Just doing a lil sight-seeing," Shonda answered, handing her the money for the temporary parking. "How're you holding up?"

"I'm about to freeze to death!" Theresa told her. "They were supposed to have fixed this heater over the weekend, but they didn't."

"So, that explains why you're wrapped up like a pig in a blanket." Shonda laughed, indicating the large coat, scarf and skull cap. Then, she glanced at her watch. "I gotta go, I'll talk to you when I get back."

"Okay, sistah," Theresa said, handing Shonda her ticket, then activating the gate to let her through.

Shonda hurriedly drove her car around the first level, looking for a parking space closer to the stairwell that led to the Underground Atlanta, to no avail. Therefore, she just chose one, and got out, clad in her large trench coat and gloves. She walked as fast as she could towards the stairwell.

On their first date, Tino had taken her to the food court, where they dined on tacos from Taco Bell, and window shopped until it was time for them to go home and get ready for school the next day.

Shonda found it coincidental that the table they'd dined at, was now unoccupied. Wasting no time, she took a seat, placed her pocketbook atop the table, and slowly surveyed the area. As her eyes darted from person to person, she began to wonder if Tino had actually flown from California, to bring her a Pyrex pot and scale. Plus, he didn't even question her request. While she was mulling over that, some guy approached, placed a box on the table, then started patting his pockets like he was looking for something.

"You're Shonda, right?" he asked, not looking in her direction.

"Yeah," she cautiously answered.

The guy asked, "What's his name?"

"Who, Tino?" she asked, not really knowing of whom he was talking about.

Well, apparently, she said what he'd wanted to hear, because as soon as she'd said Tino's name. He turned and retreated in the direction in which he'd come, leaving Shonda staring at the box he'd left as if it contained a bomb, instead of the pot and scale, or the blender that the box originally advertised. Shonda knew she couldn't just sit there and stare at the box all day. So, taking another look around, she grabbed her pocketbook and the box, then headed for the stairwell, with her heart racing, and perspiring like she was actually carrying the kilo inside the box, or a bomb.

Making it to the car, Shonda placed the box on the floor, behind the driver's seat, and took a minute to relish the cool air. She couldn't believe she'd gone into a state of panic like that, which had never happened before. Maybe it was a sign? Or, maybe it was the atmosphere, and how the whole scene had capriciously played out? Whatever it was, she was glad that she'd gotten that part out of the way.

"That didn't take long!" said Theresa, when Shonda pulled up to the booth.

"It was one of those minute-dates," Shonda joked. "He wasn't my type."

"Was it about a job?"

"You can say that," Shonda answered. "Speaking of which, I have a lot of work to do, call me later."

"Okay."

Leaving Downtown Atlanta, Shonda drove fast, but as cautious as she could, back to her apartment. Placing the box on the kitchen counter, she pulled out the glass pot, which was on top of the scale. Noticing a folded piece of paper inside the bowl, she placed the bowl on the counter and retrieved it, which was a phone number with 6:00 p.m. under it.

Shonda knew that it was a California number, by the area code. She also knew Tino not questioning her request was too good to be true. So, at six o'clock, she knew he was going to hit her with a barrage of questions, in which she felt she was obligated to answer.

****

Sheila was glad it was almost nine o'clock. She was ready to go home. She was tired, and her feet were killing her. Now, she and

Isaac, one of the male security guards, were moving boutique to boutique, making sure customers and vendors were aware of the proximity of closing time, and were making proper preparations.

"It's almost time to retire to the crib and crank that fireplace up, ain't it?" Isaac asserted as they made their rounds.

"Fireplace!" Sheila exclaimed. "You mean, central heating?"

Isaac shot her a skeptical look. "You gotta be joking! That don't even fit your description."

"And what's my description?"

"Elegant," he answered. "You seem like the type of woman that should have everything she wants, at her fingertips."

After all customers and vendors had left, Sheila made her exit, heading for her burgundy, four-door Cadillac DTS she'd obtained by trading in her Kia, and the money Shonda gave her. As she was approaching her car, she noticed the all too familiar Chevy Astro van, belonging to Tyrone from Columbus, Georgia. Who was pretty much in the mall's parking lot, every day, selling CDs and DVDs. Now, he was packing up, ready to leave.

"What did I tell you about selling stolen goods in front of the mall, Mister?" Sheila joked as she approached the passenger side of the van, where Tyrone was rummaging through his merchandise in the cargo area.

Tyrone regarded her with a broad smile. "How ya doing, Ms. Griffin?"

"I'm fine, Hustle Man," she answered, referring to him as the character from the sitcom, Martin. "What 'cha got new?"

"Nothing, really."

"What's that?" she asked, referring to the music playing inside the van.

"That's some kat named, Leroy Jackson, from Miami," he told her.

"What's the name of that song?"

"Flawda Boyz," he answered. "I ain't made no copies of it yet, but if you like it, I'll make sure to bring you a copy tomorrow. No charge!"

"No charge?"

"No charge," he repeated.
Everything has a price, Tyrone."
"That's true," he agreed. "But I feel like a queen should be exempt from having to pay for anything."
As Sheila drove home, she thought about the conversations she'd had with both, Isaac and Tyrone. She should've considered what they said to her as flattery but couldn't. On top of being a good-looking woman, a lot of men really deemed that she should be living the life of a queen. So, why wasn't she?

****

Theresa was leaving work in her blue '99 Oldsmobile Intrigue she'd leased over a week ago. As she drove, she for the umpteenth time thought about what Shonda revealed to them, Friday. She was all for *the movement* as Shonda put it, but felt she needed a little more time to think, which was why she didn't answer when Shonda asked if they were with her.

Now, looking back on how her life was back then, and how it was now. She realized she was still walking the thin line between broke and poor. It was bad enough, she didn't get a chance to go to college and get a degree in business like she wanted to. Thinking of all this, angered Theresa because she always vowed to not end up like her mother and aunt. Who worked all their lives, and were still living from check-to-check, with nothing to show for it, and here she was following that same pattern.

"I can't go out like that!" Theresa said, knowing she had to break that cycle. She knew just how she was going to do it.

****

After calming herself from the heebie-jeebies she'd developed downtown, Shonda realized she needed baking soda and Ziploc bags. Therefore, she'd driven out to the grocery store for them, and purchased a few more items, to not look suspicious.

When she returned home, her plan was to go ahead and start the process, but she hesitated. She didn't know why she was stalling, but while she was trying to figure that out, she fried herself some chicken to satisfy her hunger.

After eating and washing the dishes, she retrieved the kilo from her bedroom. Then placed it on the counter with the pot, scale, baking soda, and Ziploc bags. She was ready to begin, but after checking her watch and seeing it was almost six, she figured she'd wait until after she talked to Tino, so she could proceed without interruption. When six o'clock finally came, Shonda was sitting on the living room sofa with her cell phone in hand, and the number already programmed into it.

"Who is this?" Tino answered on the first ring.

Shonda knew enough about phones being tapped, so instead of saying her name, she asserted, "It's me."

"You found you another hustler, huh?" he asked.

"No," she answered. "Why would you say that?"

"So, the scale and pot, was for you?"

"Yeah."

"Come on Shonda," Tino said, sounding unconvinced. "You don't have to go there with me, I just want in. When he gets ready to re-up, send him my way. You know I got it."

"Well, when I get ready to re-up," she started. "I'll make sure I call you for that ex-girlfriend discount."

"That's what's up," he told her. "But why you ain't shop with me on this go-round?"

"Because, it was given to me," she answered, not willing to divulge any details on how she'd obtained the kilo. "But that's irrelevant, right now. You're my re-up man, but first, I gotta cook this stuff up. Is this your new number?"

"It's a pay phone."

"Well, I'm about to get to work," she told him. "I'll call you when I need you."

When Shonda got off the phone, she dutifully marched to the kitchen and got to work. At the same time, she was mentally putting her plan together. If Sheila, Theresa, and Ebony wouldn't take part in it, she respected their wishes. She was just going to have to do it by herself.

****

Ebony had just gotten out of the shower and was standing in front of the dressing mirror, tying her hair down, when Charles arrived home, which was minutes before nine o'clock. He said nothing as he undressed and headed for the main bathroom to take his shower. Ebony knew she shouldn't let it bother her, but she couldn't help but feel as though she was caught up in a series of reverse-role playing. One minute, Charles was all over her. Then, the next minute, he was acting like she didn't exist and vice versa.

She'd already eaten dinner and figured Charles had also so she headed for the living room. Where she was going to watch TV until she was ready for bed. As she surfed the channels, she began thinking about how much she did not want to marry Charles, and how her life would be without him. She could survive for a while off the money in her account, she'd made from the salon, but she would lose the salon. It didn't necessarily belong to her, being that it was in Charles' name.

Ebony concluded the salon was her only reason for staying because she didn't want to lose it since it was the only thing she'd ever owned that made her feel important.

****

It was after nine o'clock, Shonda had managed to cook the whole kilo in four batches. While the fourth batch was in the process of drying, she was at work at the counter, cutting, weighing and bagging ounces and half ounces. All the while, she was thinking of the rise and fall of The Kingz. She believed they'd have a longer standing if they hadn't accumulated so many enemies. She didn't know they had such enemies, until after their demise, and the media blamed them for multiple drug-related shootings resulting in a high death toll.

A knock at the front door pulled her from her reverie and startled her a bit. She wasn't expecting any company, and she was hoping it wasn't the police. Who'd probably gotten a whiff of the fumes escaping from the kitchen window, she had opened to air the apartment out.

Whoever was at the door, knocked again, causing Shonda to realize she hadn't made any effort to move. Well, she was moving now. First, she placed the Pyrex pot and scale in the cabinet under the sink. Opening the oven door, she carefully moved the newspaper that contained the dry, and almost dry substance to the oven and closed it. The ounces she'd already bagged up, she stashed in the dirty clothes hamper, then hurried to the door.

"Who is it?"

"Theresa."

Shonda found it strange that Theresa would show up without calling first, but it didn't matter, this was her friend. Plus, this could be a chance for Shonda to again try persuading her to get down with the movement.

"I was in the neighborhood and decided to stop by," Theresa asserted as if Shonda had questioned her presence.

"Bullshit!" Shonda exclaimed, smiling. "Come on in."

"What's that smell?" Theresa asked as she entered, wrinkling her nose up.

Shonda closed the door, figuring this was her chance to lay everything out on the table literally. She bided Theresa to have a seat, then fetched the bagged cocaine from the hamper, placing them on the coffee table. She, then, retrieved the product from the oven and returned to the living room, where Theresa had shed her coat and was seated on the sofa, regarding Shonda with a look of disbelief.

"Is that what I'm smelling?" Theresa asked, eyeing the product.

"Yep," she answered, kneeling on the pillow she had on the floor, beside the table.

Theresa leaned forward, now regarding Shonda from across the table. "So, you're dead ass serious, huh?"

"I understand if y'all don't wanna take that risk," Shonda said. "I'm not even mad at y'all. All I ask is for y'all to not criticize me for the life I'm about to get into. I feel like this is meant to be."

Theresa asked," Do you really believe we can pull this off?"

"There's only one way to find out," Shonda said, noting that Theresa said, "*We*."

Playa Ray

CHAPTER 14

"Who is it?"

Shonda did not expect her knock to be answered by a female's voice. She definitely hadn't driven all the way out to Summer Hill, to scuffle with a woman who may take offense, – which was highly likely – to another woman showing up on her doorsteps, asking for her man.

"Shonda," she answered, knowing she had to go on with her plan, but take a softer approach to avoid a confrontation. "I'm the girlfriend of one of Tek's friends."

It was quiet beyond the door for a few seconds. Then, Shonda heard the security locks being disengaged. When the door opened, Shonda was looking down at a dark-skin woman, who stood about 5'4", and looked to be three months pregnant. She allowed Shonda entrance, then locked the door back.

"Come on."

Shonda followed her to the living room, where Tek was seated on the sofa, with his foot up on the coffee table, talking on a cordless phone. When they entered, Tek's eyes immediately fell upon her, and his expression changed like he was trying to remember where he'd encountered her.

"Look, we'll finish this conversation, later," Tek said into the phone before hanging up. He looked back and forth from Shonda and his girlfriend before asking, "What's up?"

"She said, she's the girlfriend of one of your friends," his girl-friend answered, with no hint of attitude.

Tek shifted his gaze to Shonda. "What friend?"

"James," she answered, almost finding it hard to verbalize his name.

"James, who?"

The inflection of Tek's voice almost caused her to back out, but she remained steadfast, for the sake of her future. "King James."

"Oh, shit!" Tek exclaimed, slowing rising from the sofa, regarding Shonda like she herself was James. "I thought you looked familiar. How ya doing?"

"I'm fine."

"This is my girl, Mya," he introduced.

They nodded their regards.

"So, what brings you by?"

"I need to talk to you about something," she answered, carefully.

Tek looked as though he was recalling what she'd said, before asking Mya for some privacy. Shonda was impressed by how Mya submissively left the room when most women including herself would have been reluctant.

"Have a seat." Tek gestured to the recliner. Once she had taken a seat, Tek asked," What's up?"

"Are you still in the business?" she asked, using business as a euphemism for drug game.

"Yeah," he answered, cautiously, now sitting. "I still do my thing."

Shonda perceived how skeptical he'd become and knew she had to get straight to the point. Therefore, she pulled four Ziploc bags from her pocketbook, two ounces, and two half-ounces and placed them on the table.

"I assume you have another plug by now," Shonda started. "But if you wanna switch or know somebody that wanna cop some ounces or half-ounces for the low, I got it."

"The kats I know, are still dealing with, Drop Squad," he informed. "Some are dealing with some dude that goes by L.K.S. Ain't nobody seen him, but he got the game on smash, right now, with the best deals on the planet!"

"What kind of deals?" Shonda asked, hoping he would provide her with enough information for her to make the proper assessment, in order to compete with this guy's method.

"Is this an ounce?" Tek asked, holding up one of the bags that contained an ounce.

"Yeah."

"This is what his half-ounces look like," he told her. "Maybe just a lil smaller."

"What about, Drop Squad and their ounces?"

"They look like yours." He placed the bag back on the table. "And people are still shopping with them, knowing that L.K.S. is basically giving away dope?"

"Well, Drop Squad is really on some extortion shit," Tek told her. "You either buy from them or suffer the consequences."

Shonda already knew that about Drop Squad. She was ready to go, but she had one more question. "So, who do you shop with?"

Shonda left Tek's house, feeling as though she had not accomplished a thing, but she did manage to obtain some rather valuable information. It was good to know that Drop Squad's quantity was pretty much equal to hers. Therefore, she didn't have to alter her product, but she still hadn't thought about what to do about L.K.S., who no one had ever seen, but had the best deals on the planet, as Tek put it.

Now, she pulled into College Park Projects and parked. She had no idea if Spenz still resided there, or not, but she didn't drive all the way out here to turn back. When she approached the door and held her hand up to knock, the door swung open, startling her, and Spenz. Who apparently wasn't expecting anyone to be standing at his door, as he was – considering how he was dressed – on his way out. Now he was regarding her with the same look Tek had when she entered his living room.

"You're on your way out?" Shonda asked.

"Yeah," he answered. "I was on my way to the club. How ya been?"

"I've been okay," she told him. "You got a minute?"

"Sure, come on in."

Shonda entered the apartment, looking around. She noticed Spenz had redecorated the place.

"What's up?" Spenz asked once he'd closed the door.

"Are you still in the business?"

"Yeah," he answered. "Pills and weed."

"I figured that," she said. "I got some ounces and half-ounces of cocaine. I'll pay you for everybody you refer to me."

"What they look like?"

Shonda showed him the same product she showed Tek and told him the prices. Once he agreed to deal with her, she gave him her number and made her exit.

****

"Ms. Griffin!"

Sheila lifted her head from the control panel, to face the person that had called her name as if she'd done something wrong. When her blurry retinas adjusted and cleared, that's when she realized she had, indeed, done something wrong. She let the supervisor catch her sleeping for the second time in two weeks in the monitoring room again.

"What's your excuse, this time, Ms. Griffin?" he asked, folding his arms over his chest, and rolling his neck like the bitch he thought he was.

"Um—" She looked over at her co-worker, who pretended to be watching the monitors, and unaware of what was going on. Then, she realized that she didn't owe this fruitcake any explanation. "I was tired."

"You what!" the supervisor exclaimed, unfolding his arms, then thrusting his hands upon his hips like a true diva.

"I was tired," Sheila reiterated, standing. "As a matter of fact, I'm *still* tired!"

"Don't make me fire your ass!" he threatened. "You know you need this job!"

That was a true statement, but this nigga-bitch had struck a nerve with it. "You need this job more than I do! I got a real pussy. I don't need surgery!"

The supervisor and the other security guard, watched Sheila with enlarged pupils as she retrieved her things from her locker and marched out of the room, intentionally bumping the supervisor.

Sheila was almost to the mall's exit when someone called her name. She was not going to stop until she realized it was Isaac, the only co-worker she had allowed herself to tolerate. She turned to see him approaching at a fast pace.

"What's wrong?" he asked concerned.

"I quit."

"Why?"

"This job ain't for me," she told him, which was all she could come up with. "You just take care."

Sheila made her exit, perhaps leaving Isaac a bit heartbroken, being that he'd been trying to court her, since the day she was hired. He was a nice guy, but Sheila was not yet ready to start back dating.

The rain was coming down hard as she hurriedly headed for her car. For some reason, she expected to see Tyrone, who wouldn't let a hurricane stop him from selling his goods, in the parking lot, but two weeks ago, when he'd brought her two copies of Leroy Jackson's CD, he told her he had to head back to Columbus, Georgia, to look after his sister.

As Sheila waited for her car's heater to dispose of its cold air, she thought about what just happened. She knew, she needed the job, but there was no turning back. The damage was done. Now, she didn't think she had the energy, or the patience to go on another job hunt. She was tired of slaving, but it was the only way she would be able to pay her bills and car note. *Or was it?*

****

Ebony was now fed up with Pam's shit! Once again, the bitch had the nerve to call in, complaining of a migraine, leaving the rest of the girls to tend to her clients and a large number of walk-ins she was supposed to help with. Ebony was empathetic and considerate to her employees' afflictions and family issues, but Pam seemed to suffer one or the other, every week. Pam was a good stylist, but not good enough to keep pulling such stunts and complicating matters.

It was well after six when Ebony finished her last client. Coco was still busy with a walk-in, and Erica, who had already conducted sanitation, was lounging on the couch of the waiting area, watching the muted TV. Once Ebony let her client out, she locked the door back and began cleaning up her station.

"Erica, you could've left a long time ago," Ebony asserted while cleaning.

"Hell, I ain't got shit to do, right now," Erica replied. "My boo ain't gon' pick 'em up, until around ten."

"Why haven't I met him?"

"Because he ain't nobody special."

"Have mama met him?"

"Nope."

"Why not?"

Erica now regarded her. "Because I'm not trying to marry him. Like I said, he ain't nobody special."

Ebony didn't know why Erica was being so covert with him when she'd always been so eager to flaunt her boy toys. Maybe it had something to do with what happened between her and that guy in Chicago. Whatever it was, Ebony chose not to pry.

Once everything was done, Ebony, Erica, and Coco left the shop together. As Ebony drove home, she thought about how distant Charles had become over the past two weeks. He barely spoke to her, unless Robyn was around. Most nights, he would spend a large amount of time in the living room, watching TV, and talking on his cell. Ebony wouldn't even know if he'd slept beside her, because, when she awoke, he was already up, getting ready for work, or already gone.

Ebony thought about this until she'd pulled into the driveway, where Charles' car was already parked. For some reason, she wanted to back out of the driveway, drive off, and never look back. A blind man could see that their relationship was crumbling, and beyond repair, but the question was, How long would it be before the roof finally caved in?

Entering the house, Ebony shed her coat, then headed for the bedroom, peering into the kitchen and living room for Charles, but he wasn't in either room. When she entered the bedroom, Charles was sitting on the edge of the bed, still clad in the dress suit he'd worn to work, as if he was waiting on her. When she walked past him to place her keys and purse on the dresser, he stood.

"We need to talk," he asserted, in his serious as ever tone.

Ebony didn't know what to make of this. Her mind had instantly become cloudy. She was so nervous, she hadn't noticed that she'd taken a seat on the edge of the bed.

"T-talk about what?" she stammered.

"Our relationship."

"What about it?"

"It's not working."

Ebony was speechless. Her heart felt as though it had stopped beating, as tears threatened to cascade down her face. Charles continued. "You can't be that naïve to not have noticed. Lately, we've just been going through the motions. What we had is gone, and I feel we should go ahead and do what we have to do. You can keep the car and the engagement ring. I'll help you find a place to stay. If you want me to, I'll pay for it."

"What about the salon?" Ebony asked, feeling selfish once the words escaped her lips, but holding her breath as she anticipated his answer.

At first, Charles looked as though he had not thought of the salon. Then, as if he'd come up with a bright idea, he said, "I'll hold on to it."

Those five words shattered Ebony's world. Hell, she would have given him back the car, engagement ring and every piece of jewelry and clothing he'd bought her, to keep the shop. She couldn't believe he'd actually stripped her of the best thing that ever happened to her.

Ebony wanted so bad to protest, but her pride forbade her. She also wanted to lunge at Charles and beat some kind of sense into him, and truth be told, she couldn't think of one thing that was holding her back from doing so. Therefore, not knowing how much longer she could hold herself back, she gracefully lifted from the bed, retrieved her purse and keys from the dresser, and, with her head held high, brushed past Charles, headed for the front door. As she passed him, she noticed that he reeked of the same perfume she'd smelled on his shirt she'd found in the dirty clothes hamper. The same perfume that she was highly familiar with.

****

It was only 7:30, and Shonda was bored out of her mind. She could not believe she was sitting on the living room couch, staring beyond the television, in lieu of paying attention to the images on the screen, being that she had a lot on her mind. She was still wondering how she was going to build her clientele. She had almost talked herself into calling Tino and asking him to plug her in with some local drug dealers in Georgia, that he was still in contact with. The more she thought about it, the bigger the urge to do it had become.

"Fuck it!" she said to herself, grabbing her cell phone off the table.

Shonda brought herself to realize, by doing this, she had nothing to lose, but much to gain. Before she could dial the fourth digit of Tino's number, there was a knock on her door. Taking it as a sign, she remitted the call and headed for the door.

"Who is it?"

"Room service."

Recognizing Theresa's voice, Shonda opened the door to see that she was accompanied by Sheila. She bided them to enter and took their coats as they settled in the living room.

"Y'all want something to drink, or eat?" Shonda asked, noticing they both conveyed parallel solemn looks on their faces. They shook their heads.

After placing their coats on her bed, Shonda returned to the living room and sat in the recliner, being that her guests were occupying the sofa.

"Why the long faces?" Shonda pried, hoping to find out why her friends had shown up at her apartment, unexpectantly, and looking hopeless.

Theresa answered, "We're unemployed, and on the brink of knocking over a bank."

"Hold on, Cleo!" Shonda exclaimed, referring to her as the character *Queen Latifah* played on the movie, '*Set It Off.*'

"Girl, you still got a job!" Sheila said, regarding Theresa as if she wasn't quite sure of what she had just said.

"Today was my last day," replied Theresa. "I put in my two weeks' notice, two weeks ago."

Sheila appeared shocked. "Why?"

"I think I have a better calling," Theresa answered, regarding Shonda.

"And what brings *you* to the unemployment line?" Shonda asked Sheila, already feeling things were about to go as she'd planned.

"I quit my job," Sheila answered, then explained the minor confrontation she had with her supervisor.

"So, is it official?" Shonda asked, after hearing Sheila's story. "Do I count y'all in?"

"Hell yeah!" came Theresa.

"I'm in," said Sheila. "You'll have to run the whole game plan by me again. Make sure you include all profit and benefits."

"Well, first—"

Before Shonda could convey her plan to her girls, there was another knock on the door. She didn't know who it could be, but she was ready to send them on their way, so she could get back to business.

"Who is it?" she asked, approaching the door.

"Ebony."

Shonda was, again, surprised. She didn't know what to think about all her girls showing up at her place, on the same night, unannounced. When she opened the door, she noticed Ebony appeared more distraught than Sheila and Theresa did.

"What's wrong, baby?" Shonda asked, already seeing the tears well up in her eyes.

"He left me!" Ebony wailed, letting the tears flow as she wept uncontrollably.

Shonda's heart churned for her friend as she grabbed her by the hands, pulled her in out of the cold and embraced her. Sheila and Theresa joined them, both taking turns consoling their friend. Once

Ebony calmed down, they escorted her to the sofa, got her a glass of water, and listened patiently as she told her story.

"I can't believe he took the salon from me!" Ebony asserted again, fumbling with the engagement ring on her finger.

"We should burn that muthafuckah down!" Theresa vented. "He ain't gon' do nothing but give it to another bitch!"

"That's what you wanna do, Ebony?" Shonda asked, ready to do whatever it, took to give her friend closure.

Ebony looked around at her friends before answering, "Of course, I wanna burn it down, but that won't change nothing. I still won't have it."

"Hell, at least another bitch won't have it," Theresa persisted.

"Theresa!" Shonda had to intervene because she knew Theresa was going to push until Ebony changed her mind. Right now, Shonda needed to know if Ebony was down with the movement. "So, what 'cha gonna do about work?" she asked Ebony.

Ebony shrugged. "I don't know."

"I still got that key," Shonda told her. "It's already cooked and bagged up. We don't wanna do it without you, but—"

"*We?*" Ebony looked from Theresa to Sheila.

"The only person missing, is you," Shonda asserted.

Ebony gave it some thought before asking, "What am I supposed to do?"

"There's no I in team," Shonda said. "But being that we only have ounces and half-ounces, with no customers yet. I think we should break some of it down into tens and twenties and set up shop to get some money coming in. Sheila and Theresa, y'all set up shop where y'all at. Ebony, I assume you'll be staying with me for the time being. We'll hold it down out here. This will be the stash house. Everything made, comes back here. We're just starting, so our commission won't be much, but it'll be enough for bills and car notes. We just have to make this stuff sell. We can make it work. It just won't happen overnight. If y'all—"

Shonda stopped to retrieve her ringing cell phone off the table. The unfamiliar number on the screen made her not want to answer, but something told her to do so. It was Spenz, telling her that he had two guys that wanted to each cop an ounce. Delighted, she hooked the meeting up for tomorrow, at Spenz' place, since he knew them, and was getting a hundred dollars per customer referred.

"We got two customers," Shonda said, once she got off the phone. "Two ounces, all Queenz have to be present."

****

"Park right there," Shonda, who was seated on the passenger side of Sheila's Cadillac, said, pointing to a parking space in the parking lot of College Park Projects.

They had all assembled at Shonda's apartment, at ten o'clock, and driven out to Gwinnett County to get Ebony's things. Charles wasn't home, and, unlike most women, Ebony conducted herself like a lady, gathering her things, leaving the keys on the dresser, and exiting without sabotaging, or taking anything that didn't belong to her although she did think about going with Theresa's advice of throwing Charles' clothes in a tub full of bleach. Leaving there, they journeyed to the salon, where Ebony had sent Sheila inside to retrieve her things. Erica didn't show up to work, because Ebony called her last night and told her what happened.

Now, they all dismounted the Cadillac and were heading towards DJ Spenz' apartment. Shonda had a .380 that James bought her, and taught her how to shoot, but being that she would be conducting the deal, and the Army had classified Theresa as a *Weapons Specialist*, she decided to let Theresa tote the gun.

"Come on in," Spenz said, looking a bit surprised that Shonda was not alone.

They entered to see two guys seated on the sofa. Shonda didn't have a bad vibe, but she'd told her girls they were going to make this quick as possible.

"Let me see the money!" Shonda demanded, standing across the table from them. They both pulled out a wad of bills. "Put it on the table!"

They complied. Shonda retrieved the money, handing one wad to Sheila, and the other to Ebony, who both counted the bills. Once they'd confirmed the amount, Shonda pulled the scale from her large pocketbook. Then, she pulled out one of the ounces, extracted it from the Ziploc, and placed it on the scale for the first guy.

"So, y'all are The Kingz widows, huh?" the first guy asked.

Shonda stared at him, not knowing how, or if she should answer the question, being that The Kingz had multiple enemies. That's when she realized how easy it was for them to fall into the trap of someone who's still bitter because they didn't get the pleasure of killing The Kingz themselves.

"Niggas were hating on The Kingz!" the second guy spoke. "Them boys had shit on lock."

"Yeah, them boys did they thang!" the first guy chimed in. To Shonda, he said, "They opened the doors for y'all. It's up to y'all to keep that legacy going."

CHAPTER 15

It was now June, it seemed as though six months had shot by in only weeks. The girls had managed to accumulate a decent clientele. It seemed people wanted to deal with them because they were the *Kingz Widows*. Some claimed they were paying homage, or supporting the cause, which was more than they could ask for or more than either one of them had expected. Even when they were out people who recognized them, would greet them and give their condolences.

Now, Shonda was leaving the jewelry store and on her way to the house that she and Sheila shared in Norcross, Georgia. It was Friday, and their supply was low, but the two kilos Shonda ordered from Tino, wouldn't arrive until Tuesday. She had to use money from her account, but it was worth it, and she still hadn't heard a word on Mario.

"I just can't win with you, huh?"

Shonda burst into laughter. Doolu had been trying to get with her since they'd met at the tire shop in Savannah. When she had to pick up her car that Mario had taken and abandoned. When she'd called him in February, she apologized for the three months it took to do so. Once, he accepted her apology, she told him what she and her girls were doing, and he supported the cause by introducing them to a few customers and copping a few ounces himself. Now she knew that this wasn't about business, because he was calling her cell phone, and not the phone at the house that was set up for business purposes only.

"What's your order?" she asked, feeling a bit playful.

"Shit, I want the Queen Shonda special," Doolu answered. "Tonight, if possible."

"I'm sorry," Shonda said, smiling. "That is not possible."

"You just won't let me win, will you?"

"There's no fun in just *letting* you win."

"So, I have to be of a certain status, huh?"

"No," she answered, knowing he was referring to King James. "My friends and I are throwing a Fourth of July party, next month.

147

We haven't figured out what club or park we'll have it at, but I'll send you an invitation if you'd like to attend.

"That's almost three weeks from now!" he protested.

"So, no invitation for you?"

"Girl, I better be the first one on the list!" he asserted. "And when are y'all gonna get some of that green stuff? Niggas be looking for that shit too."

Doolu was right. On several occasions, guys had inquired about marijuana, thinking The Queenz were running The Kingz full operation. This let her know she had a phone call to make, as soon as she got home.

Shonda pulled into the empty driveway that indicated, Sheila had not made it home from her hair appointment, which was good. She could sneak the things that she'd bought from the jewelry store, into the house, without being seen and having to explain what they were before it was time. She managed to hide the four, gift-wrapped boxes in her closet. After checking for messages on the business phone, she dialed Spenz' number and took a seat at the kitchen table, while the lines connected.

"What up?" Spenz answered.

"You busy?" she asked.

"Nah," he answered. "Y'all ain't thought about what club y'all gon' have Theresa's birthday party?"

"Nope," Shonda was smiling. Spenz was crazy about Theresa, so she already knew what he about to suggest.

"Man, y'all might as well come on to the spot," he suggested like Shonda knew he would. "We ain't had no major action, since The Kingz."

"I'll think about it," she told him. "I called you for another reason."

"What's that?"

"I need you to turn me on to your plug."

"You trying to get some weed?"

"And some x-pills," she said. "If it's not too much to ask, who is this connect.?"

"L.K.S."

148

"What, why you ain't tell me you were dealing with this dude?"

"You ain't never ask."

"Have you ever met him?"

"Nah," he answered. "You know him?"

"I've been hearing about him," she said. "Who turned you on to him?"

"He contacted me."

"L.K.S.?"

"He sent one of his lieutenants," Spenz answered. "Some dude with an up North accent. He approached me at the club one night and told me that the employer wanted to front me some work."

"Why you?"

"I don't know. He said his employer was a real close friend of my last employer."

"And who was your last employer?"

"King James."

****

"You're done ma'am."

Ebony looked up from the old Kings magazine that she had busied herself with for over an hour, while her car was being detailed. The guy that had spoken, was wearing sunglasses, which made it hard to decipher if he was talking to her, or the other woman that was present.

"White Infiniti, right?" he asked.

"Yeah." Ebony got up, placed the magazine in the chair, and followed the guy out of the office building, into the warm summer breeze.

Ebony had never had her car detailed before and being that she no longer had Charles to wash it, she had to make it happen. Now, her car looked brand-new, and the interior conveyed a sweet smell that was indescribable.

"You waxed the seats too?" Ebony asked, feeling how slippery the leather seat was beneath her.

"I wiped it down with Armor-All," he told her. "It won't rub off on your clothes."

"Sixty dollars, right?" she asked, rummaging through her purse.

"Yeah," he answered, then asked. "Why are all the fine women always taken?"

The question caught her off guard. "What makes you think I'm taken?" she asked, handing him the money.

"The ring," he said. "Unless you wear it to keep men at bay."

"I don't need a ring for that," Ebony told him. "I know how to turn a man down. As for the ring, I was engaged to be married. Apparently, he had other plans."

"He let you slip through his fingers like that?"

"Things happen," she said, starting the car. "I have to get going."

Before he could respond, she closed the driver's door, and drove out of the parking lot, thinking of how she'd only had sex with one man, since the break-up with Charles. It was a one-night stand, which was all she would allow because she was not willing to let another man drag her through the mud as though she was worthless.

Ebony pulled up to the house that she shared with Theresa in Riverdale and parked beside Theresa's car. Theresa must've been looking out the window because she opened the front door as Ebony approached.

"You ain't been out stalking, have you?" Theresa asked, smiling.

"I been gave that up," Ebony answered, knowing that Theresa was talking about the times Ebony had driven by the salon to see if there was a new girl, or by Charles office and home to see if she would catch him with someone.

"Yeah, right," Theresa asserted, following Ebony to her room. "I talked to Shonda, she asked me if I wanted my party at Strokers."

"At a strip club?" Ebony asked, entering her room and dropping her purse on the bed.

"I'm cool with it," said Theresa, leaning against the door jam. "We ain't never had a problem with going to Strokers."

"True," Ebony now regarded her friend. "It's gonna be at Strokers?"

"Absolutely!"

****

It was Saturday and the girls were gathered in the parking lot of the shooting range, where they frequented every other Saturday. Shonda was the only one who wasn't eligible for a gun permit, but it didn't stop her from carrying. They'd done their shooting routine for the day and were ready to leave.

"What're y'all about to do?" Shonda asked Ebony and Theresa, being that they'd rode together like she and Sheila had.

"McCoy's Bar and Grill," Ebony answered.

"I heard they got some good food," said Sheila. "You wanna join them, Shonda?"

"I'm exhausted," Shonda answered. "My plan was to go home and take a long nap, but you can join them if you want."

"Y'all gon' take me home?" Sheila asked them.

"Hell no!" Ebony answered. "We'll give you bus fare."

"Or call you a cab," Theresa chimed in.

"You gon' be alright?" Sheila asked Shonda.

"As soon as I get some rest."

Sheila rode off with Theresa and Ebony, and Shonda drove home. When she entered the house, it wasn't her intentions to check the messages on the business phone, but she did anyway. There was a message from Clarence, stating that he didn't get his ounce, yesterday. That's when she realized they'd forgot to make that drop. After checking the stash and seeing that they only had a few half-ounces left. She called Clarence and told him she could accommodate him with two halves.

"They proper?" he asked.

"We haven't let you down yet," she told him. "See you in thirty?"

"I'm there."

Shonda was not happy that she had to make this drive, when she could be resting, and shouldn't be making this drop by herself, but it had to be done. They'd been dealing with Clarence since March, and all deals had been conducted in an orderly fashion. Therefore, she didn't have any bad vibes about this run.

Getting off on the Howell Mill Road exit, Shonda pulled into the Kroger's parking lot, parking a respectable distance from the black Acura. Ready to get it over with, she quickly dismounted, headed for the car, and climbed into the passenger seat.

"That was my fault," Shonda said, apologetically. "I don't know how I skipped you like that."

"It's all good," Clarence said, taking a long pull on his blunt before sitting it in the ashtray and pulling a wad of bills from under his seat. "Where's the rest of The Queenz?"

"They went out to lunch," she answered, retrieving the two halves from her purse, and handing them to him, exchanging for the money.

Shonda didn't feel as though she needed to count the money, but it was all part of business. She was half-way through the bills when the report from a gun filled the car. The sound startled her, but the blood that splattered on the left side of her face, caused her to freeze up. That's when she knew she had been shot.

Now, her mind was racing. She'd just handed Clarence the co-caine. When she looked down to count the money, Clarence was opening the Ziploc to inspect his product. Shonda didn't consider herself to be the smartest person in the world, but she was quite sure, in order for him to manage to shoot her in the short span of time that he did, he would have had to already had the gun in his hand, which he didn't. Or, maybe the gun in her purse had discharged accidentally.

Well, she didn't have to wonder any longer. The constant sound of the car's horn brought her out of her trance. That's when she re-alized she wasn't the one who'd been shot. Someone had shot Clar-ence in the head, which was why he was leaning on the steering wheel, but before she could make any more sense of the situation. The passenger door swung open, and she was snatched out of the car by her hair and forced to the ground. A kick to her abdomen, caused her to double over, but that was just the beginning.

Another pair of legs – which was all she could see – had approached. When the first guy raised his foot, Shonda put up her arms to shield her face, although her ribs were his intended target. All she could do was ball up as they kicked and stomped her. The blows were fierce, and the pain was severe, but Shonda held in her screams. She would not give them the pleasure of knowing they were hurting her.

Once the assault ceased, one of the goons asserted, "If you don't wanna end up like ya boyfriend, find another occupation!"

Then, all she heard was the sound of their shoes as they ran off in the direction of Taco Bell and Arby's. Of course, the car's loud-ass horn was still blaring, which was probably the only thing that was keeping her from blacking out.

Shonda was in so much pain, she wanted to lie there until some-one found her. Then, realization kicked in, a man was just murdered in front of her. His blood was all over her, she had a gun in her purse; and— hell, that was enough to force her eyes open and mus-ter enough strength to pull herself into a crawling position. When her eyes gained focus, she saw that her purse was near, but the bloodied bills had been scattered by the light summer breeze.

Looking around, she saw that there was a small crowd of people standing in front of Kroger's, which was over a hundred yards from where she was. She knew that, unless they had a birds-eye-view or binoculars, there was no way they could read the license plate of her car that was only a few yards away.

Reaching her purse, Shonda willed her aching body off the ground, and staggered towards her car, with one hand clutching her purse, and the other one clutching her side. She wouldn't dare bid herself another look at Clarence's body. More than happy she'd left her keys in the ignition, Shonda started the car and bailed out of the parking lot as if *she* was responsible for what had just taken place.

****

"What up ladies!"

Theresa, Sheila, and Ebony had been at McCoy's Bar and Grill for over two hours, eating, drinking, dancing, and just enjoying themselves. Now, as they sat at their table, enjoying another round of drinks, they were regarding three men that had approached.

"Can we join y'all?" the guy asked, revealing a mouthful of gold teeth.

"There's only one empty chair," Ebony asserted, hoping they'd get the hint because she definitely wasn't in the mood to be bothered by some no good men that only had one thing on their minds.

"Shit, we can grab some more chairs," another guy that was wearing a Drop Squad chain, offered.

"Um, before you take it upon yourself to invade our happy hour," Theresa started. "How old are y'all?"

"Shit, we're some grown ass men!" Drop Squad answered.

"A grown man does not walk around with his pants hanging off his ass," Theresa replied. "That does not impress classy women, such as us. To answer your question, no, you cannot join us. Thanks, anyway."

For a second, the men regarded each other with confused expressions, like they were trying to figure out if they should take offense to Theresa's remark.

"Man, let's bounce!" the third guy finally spoke. "These hoes ain't talkin' 'bout shit!"

"Was it something I said?" Theresa asked her friends, once the men had walked away, causing laughter.

"I think you handled that well," Sheila commented. "Hell, you handled it better than Shonda would have."

"Oh, hell yeah!" Theresa agreed. "Fucking with Shonda, we would've had to whoop them niggas' asses!"

"Straight up!" Ebony agreed, laughing. "Hey, I'm ready to leave whenever y'all are."

"I'm ready," said Theresa. "We may have to wait on Sheila's cab."

"You know what?" Sheila started, "I was about to say that I was gonna kick your ass, but then I remembered you ain't got no ass."

"She ain't got no ass?" Ebony asked, instigating.

"Hell no!" Sheila fed into it. "But if I ever need an ironing board, I know where to look."

"Girl, my ass ain't that damn flat!" Theresa asserted, laughing.

They finally left the Bar and Grill, en route to Norcross. Sheila thought to call and see if Shonda wanted something to eat but remembering Shonda's plan was to go home and nap, she dismissed the thought and still ordered her cousin a plate to go.

Getting home, Sheila entered the house and headed for the kitchen where she placed Shonda's plate into the microwave, then headed for the bathroom. As soon as she entered the bathroom, she was hit by a strong stench of bleach, as if the bathroom had just been cleaned. Forcing herself to endure the smell, she proceeded to drain her bladder. While washing her hands, she noticed something that looked like smeared blood, on the edge of the sink. Being that it was almost unnoticeable, Sheila didn't give it a second thought but washed it away with one of her soapy fingers.

Leaving the bathroom, Sheila stopped and peered into Shonda's bedroom, to see that she was wrapped up in her bedspread, fast asleep. Closing the door back, Sheila eased off to her own room, where she kicked off her shoes and climbed on top of her bed to take a nap herself.

When she awoke, she saw that it had gotten dark. Remembering she didn't leave a note on the microwave to let Shonda know that the food belonged to her. Sheila got out of bed and first went to check on Shonda. Shonda's bedroom door was open, and she was not in her bed. The sound of water running led Sheila to the kitchen where Shonda, clad in shorts and a long-sleeved, button-down shirt, was washing some dishes in the sink. Sheila was about to enter but stopped short of the entrance. She instantly noticed something disturbing about Shonda's posture.

Shonda, whose back was to Sheila, moved towards the refrigerator at a slow pace, clutching her side. When she opened the door of the refrigerator, she winced, which was followed by a painful grunt. This made Sheila think about the smeared blood on the sink.

Now, Sheila entered. "Girl, what's wrong with you?"

"Nothing," Shonda answered, keeping her back turned. "Hungry as hell!"

"I brought you a plate back," Sheila said, standing on the other side of the counter. "It's in the microwave."

Shonda closed the door, turned, and moved towards the microwave. That's when Sheila noticed that the left side of Shonda's face was a bit swollen, and her bottom lip pierced. Plus, her face was caked with makeup, as if she was trying to hide it. Sheila knew it would be futile to question her about it, so she headed for the bathroom to conduct her business.

CHAPTER 16

It was Tuesday, and The Queenz were en route to meet Leon, one of Tino's workers, in the black GMC Denali that they'd bought to accommodate them on their business runs. Ebony, who was driving the truck, exited off on South Cobb Drive and drove to the Knights Inn Motel. They already knew what room Leon was in. So, once Ebony found a parking spot, they all took a minute to survey the area and check the guns in their pocketbooks before dismounting and heading towards the door.

Shonda, whose side was still hurting from Saturday's ordeal, did her best to walk as upright as she could, although the pain was trying to force her into a standing fetal position. She initiated the special knock, then shoved her hand inside her pocketbook, gripping her gun like the others.

Seconds later, Leon opened the door, allowing them in. Shonda stood beside Leon, while Theresa checked the bathroom. Sheila checked under the bed and Ebony positioned herself by the window to keep watch.

"I like the way y'all work!" Leon commented, closing the door, and pulling two kilos from a gray bag on the bed, placing them side by side.

Shonda produced her pocketknife to test the product. Once she was content, she paid Leon, then handed the kilos to Theresa and Sheila, who each stuffed one inside their pocketbooks.

"I heard about the birthday party," said Leon. "If I wanna fall through, what would I need, an invitation?"

"Just thirty dollars," Shonda answered.

"Thirty dollars?"

"That'll cover the food and drinks," Shonda told him. "Make sure you get there before it gets too crowded."

The Queenz left Cobb County and made it back to Norcross, where they all assembled at Shonda and Sheila's house which was the stash house. Shonda, who'd obtained another Pyrex pot, began breaking the kilos down and started the cooking process with the help of Theresa. Once the first batch was done and hardened, Sheila and Ebony began cutting, weighing, and bagging up ounces. Being that the other kilo was to be converted into half-ounces, and would take longer, Theresa and Shonda had to assist Ebony and Sheila.

"What made you get the car painted?" Ebony asked Shonda as they tended to the cocaine at the kitchen table.

"I guess it was time for a new look," Shonda answered. She'd taken the Mustang to a paint shop, yesterday, and had got it back this morning, with its new highly-polished black coat, which put her at ease, just in case witnesses had mentioned anything about a red Mustang to the authorities, and they'd put out an APB. Shonda had seen Clarence's incident on the news. The reporters neither mentioned his name or anything about a suspected Ford Mustang.

Shonda was also relieved that the bruises on her arms and the cut on her lip were healing and barely noticeable. Although she still applied a light application of foundation to her arms. She had also taken money from her account to cover Clarence's order so that the books would add up.

After the cocaine was bagged up and stored away, Shonda called an immediate Queenz meeting. The girls protested, complaining to be tired and hungry, but Shonda persisted, assuring them it would only take ten minutes. Once they had all complied to her, Shonda went to her room, retrieved the four boxes she'd brought from the jewelry store, and returned to the kitchen, placing one in front of each of them.

"Y'all can go ahead and open 'em," Shonda told them, retaking her seat, where her own box sat.

Shonda watched as they opened their boxes and pulled out gold, diamond-encrusted tiaras, and closely looked them over with parallel admiration. This made Shonda more than happy to pull hers out and place it on her head.

"We're already known as The Queenz," Shonda spoke. "As of now, neither one of us has declined that title. We accept it. These tiaras are for added measure. They'll give us that official stand if I'm saying it right. The Kingz wore crowns, which made them stand out and boosted their reputation. Nobody ruled over nobody, every decision was unanimous."

"So, that's pretty much how we should run our operation," said Sheila.

"We've already been running it like that," Shonda replied. "These tiaras are the main objectives of this meeting. It's decision-making time. I need to know if The Queenz are going to accept these royal gifts, or not, Queen Theresa?"

"You don't have to ask me," Theresa answered, putting hers on.

"Queen Sheila?"

"As long as it don't mess up my hair," Sheila asserted, donning hers.

"Queen—" Shonda started, but Ebony was already positioning hers atop her head. "So, it's official, but I do have one more suggestion before I let y'all go. I was thinking we should switch our wardrobe up some. Try the casual approach from time to time."

"I've been thinking the same thing," said Theresa. "We need to take on the businesswoman's look."

****

"He damn sho' picked a fine time to re-up!" Theresa grumbled, still upset they had to make a drop, on her birthday, which was the day of her party.

The Queenz were on the highway, en route to Lagrange, to drop off two ounces to Fo 'Pound, someone who was introduced to them through Doolu. They'd spent all day preparing for tonight, starting at the massage parlor, migrating to a hair salon, and ending at a nail salon. It was almost eight o'clock and being that the party would officially begin at ten. They'd taken the initiative to get dressed, with the intent to leave Lagrange, and head straight for Club Strokers.

"It's all part of doing business," Shonda who was driving the truck, now replied to Theresa's muttering. "It's still your birthday, and the party still don't start until we get there."

"You're right," Theresa, who was seated in the rear with Ebony, agreed.

Shonda pulled the truck off on the Lagrange exit and headed for the designated area, which was a forest-like setting that sat behind some apartments, which they assumed Fo 'Pound resided. As always, he and his friend were leaning against the same tree, smoking a blunt.

Shonda parked about ten yards from them, then looked back at Theresa. Who was to remain in the truck, close to the AK-47 that sat in the rear compartment behind the seats. Shonda felt it was time they beefed up their firepower a little. Plus, she'd advised that they start carrying throw-away Glocks.

"Go for it!" Theresa responded to Shonda's inquisitive look.

"Let's get it!" Shonda asserted, grabbing the brown paper bag that contained the cocaine, then dismounted, followed by Sheila and Ebony.

They all stood a few feet in front of the truck, with Ebony and Sheila both flanking Shonda at a short distance, keeping watch, while gripping the guns in their pocketbooks.

"I like the new look!" Fo 'Pound asserted as he and his friend approached.

"Thank you," Shonda replied, figuring he was referring to their tiaras and change in attire. She handed him the bag. "Same product."

"I can dig it," he replied, handing her the money. "The Birthday Girl didn't wanna get out?"

"That's her post," Shonda told him. "Plus, she's a bit agitated that we had to come out here."

"Damn, my bad!"

"It's all business. Y'all coming through?"

"I got a family to feed."

"I feel that," Shonda told him. "You know the number."

The Queenz climbed back into the truck and were on their way back to Atlanta.

"Y'all know what?" Sheila asked once they were back on the highway. "I think we should all get the same kind of cars like The Kingz did."

"We ain't got it like that yet," Shonda told her.

"We may not be able to buy the cars, right now," Sheila persisted. "But I'm quite sure we have enough money to lease them."

"What kind of cars?" Theresa asked, interested.

Sheila answered, "BMW M-3 convertibles."

"Those are some nice cars!" Ebony voiced.

"Can we, at least, wait and see what kind of deal L.K.S. is gonna give us on the weed and pills?" Shonda asked.

She'd asked DJ Spenz to negotiate for her and planned to get a reply tonight.

It was shortly after ten when Shonda pulled the GMC into the crowded parking lot of Strokers. She managed to maneuver the truck to the front of the club, where there was a reserved parking spot for them. Shonda rolled the tinted window down on the passenger side. Once one of the security guards acknowledged them, he removed the reserved sign, so they could park.

"Do we leave our guns?" Ebony wanted to know.

"Nope," Shonda answered, sternly.

She didn't have a clue who her assailants were, but if they decided to half-way reveal themselves tonight, she was going to make sure she and her girls were ready.

When they'd dismounted, cheers and applause erupted from the crowd of people outside the club, which was surprising to them. Almost by instinct, they regarded them with smiles and waves as they headed for the entrance where security greeted them, and one led them inside towards the VIP booth.

"Ahh shit!" DJ Spenz spouted over the music. "The Birthday Girl has finally arrived. I repeat, the Birthday Girl has finally arrived, and that could only mean one thing. The Queenz are in the building! Y'all give it up for the lovely, and beautiful Queenz!"

The crowd regarded them as the outside crowd did, and The Queenz showed their appreciation. The club owner was standing by the booth when they approached.

"Hello ladies!" he greeted them. "Should I go ahead and put everything in motion?"

Everybody looked at Theresa.

"I don't see why not," Theresa said, seeing that it was her call.

"And leave him with us," Shonda told the owner, indicating the bouncer that had escorted them in.

"I can do that," he replied. "Anything else?"

"Yeah," Shonda answered. "Don't get lost!"

The owner left, and The Queenz entered the booth where there were four wooden chairs with royal blue cushions, lined along the wall. A small table sat on the right side of each chair, containing ice buckets, bottles of Patron, and craftily designed drinking glasses. They took their seat and looked out at the crowd that was slowly growing. The catering service had set up shop beside the bar and had the place smelling like a soul food restaurant. Strippers were conducting their routine lap dances, and two were entertaining from the stage.

"This must be for decoration?" Sheila asked, pointing at the small table beside her chair. "Y'all know I don't drink strong alcohol no more."

"It's for decoration," Shonda said, now remembering that her cousin had pretty much given up on alcohol a few months ago. "I'll make sure to get you something to drink when they get here with the food."

As she said it, they saw that the manager and some of the caterers were on their way with the table and food dishes. As they set up the table and dishes, claiming they had to retrieve the rest of the food. Shonda told the manager to make sure Sheila was provided with non-alcoholic beverages, which is why he brought her back a large bottle of Tropicana orange juice. Once the food was placed, they dug in, feasting on hot wings, buffalo wings, potato wedges, sliced turkey and cheese, and celery sticks with blue cheese dip.

While she ate, Ebony pondered her thoughts of calling a Queenz meeting and expressing to them her thoughts of approaching Charles and asking him if he would sell the salon to her. However, the more she thought about it, the more she thought against it.

"How's the food, Queenz?" Shonda asked.

"It's good," answered Theresa.

Ebony agreed.

"I gotta piss!" said Sheila.

"Let's go," Shonda said, being that she and Sheila were each other's personal security, which was the same with Ebony and Theresa.

Sheila and Shonda grabbed their pocketbooks and exited the booth. Theresa and Ebony watched as they moved through the crowd, hugging and shaking hands with some of the people that seemed to be happy to meet them.

"So, I guess we're what they call hood celebrities, huh?" Ebony asked as she watched the scene.

"Basically," Theresa answered. "I like it."

"Yeah, me, too."

Shonda and Sheila followed the female bartender into the ladies' restroom, where she had to unlock the reserved stall for them.

"I have to wait for y'all to finish, so I can lock it back," the bartender instructed and she did just that. Once they used the stall, they washed their hands, then exited.

"I wanna stop by the booth and holla at Spenz real quick," Shonda told Sheila.

Sheila nodded. They headed for the DJ booth, which seemed like an eternity to reach. As they were constantly greeted by more admirers. When they finally reached the booth, they were greeted by the two guys that worked for Spenz. One asked if they wanted to buy weed, and the other asked if they wanted to buy pills.

"Nope," Shonda answered, pushing past them and entering the booth, leaving Sheila standing outside.

"What's wrong?" Spenz asked with a puzzled look on his face.

"Nothing yet," she answered. "What's the word on that?"

"Ain't nobody fell through yet," he told her. "When they do, I'll let you know."

When they'd made it back to the booth, it was Ebony and Theresa's turn to take a restroom break. Shonda and Sheila watched as they moved through the crowd the same way, hugging and shaking hands, which Shonda now realized was quite dangerous, but not as dangerous as the five guys that had now blocked Ebony and Theresa's path, all sporting Drop Squad chains.

Shonda and Sheila exchanged quick glances, acknowledging they both were witnessing the same thing. Looking back at the scene, they saw that Theresa and one of the guys were swapping words for a moment before Theresa, literally, plowed through them, with Ebony in tow. The Drop Squad members proceeded on like nothing had transpired. The guy Theresa swapped words with, approached a light-skinned, blonde dancer, who was giving someone a lap dance and said something in her ear that made her jilt her customer and follow him and his crew to a table where she climbed on top and began entertaining them.

Watching them, made Shonda wonder for the billionth time if Drop Squad was responsible for Clarence's death, and her assault. She was also wondering why Spenz had not announced their arrival. On top of that, she was anticipating her friends' return, because she was extremely anxious to hear what this guy said to Theresa.

"Excuse me ladies!" the club owner entered the booth, handing Sheila another bottle of orange juice. "Pardon my intrusion. I just wanted to know if y'all were ready for the cake?"

"In twenty minutes," Shonda told him.

The owner looked at this watch, then exited. That's when Shonda spotted Theresa and Ebony emerging from the restroom, making their way back to the booth.

"What did Drop Squad want?" Shonda asked Theresa as soon as they sat down.

"Dude introduced himself as, Rico," Theresa answered, taking a sip of her Patron. "He wanted to know where we're getting our work from, and who's cooking it for us."

"And what did you tell him?"

"That it was none of his damn business!"

Shonda thought about this a little more as they continued eating. Now, she was watching their table. That's when she noticed that the dancer was more interested in them than Drop Squad. The catering service workers entering the booth had adverted her attention. They had brought in the cake and were collecting the food dishes while singing 'Happy Birthday' to Theresa. Who was doing her best not to smile. Once the song was over, Theresa blew out the twenty-seven candles, and cut her and her girls a piece of cake. The caterers exited the booth, right as Spenz was entering, carrying a small, black jewelry box.

"Happy Birthday!" he said, handing her the box across the table.

Theresa opened it and pulled out a small platinum chain that had a platinum diamond-encrusted 'T' hanging from it. "It's beautiful!" she exclaimed, standing, and rounding the table to hug him. "Thank you!"

"You're welcome. You want me to put it on?"

She handed the necklace to him, then turned so that he could put it on, which he did quite gracefully, with a bit of seduction.

"Thank you!" she said again, now looking into his eyes.

"What you got planned for tonight?" he asked.

"Nothing special."

"I brought my protégé with me tonight," he told her. "He's my backup DJ. If you want to, we can get a room and—"

"Whoa, Kemosabe!" Theresa cut him off. "Get a room?"

"I mean, I don't think my place is appropriate," he told her. "I think a nice hotel room would be more suitable and relaxing. I just want your company. Whatever we do, is up to you, it's your call."

Theresa was already aware that Spenz had the hots for her, and she also found him to be quite charming. That didn't mean she was just going to jump in the bed with him like some random street walker. She was a Queen, for crying out loud!

"Not tonight," she finally answered. "I do appreciate the offer."

Not wanting to leave him feeling as though he'd been rejected, she hugged him and planted a kiss on his jaw.

"That was so sweet!" Ebony said, once Spenz left, and Theresa retook her seat.

"Girl, why you ain't give that man no booty?" asked Sheila. "You know you ain't had no dick since you've been back."

"And whose problem is that?" Theresa countered.

"All of ours," Sheila answered. "Cause, if you don't get no dick any time soon. You might start looking at Ebony, with her thick, fine ass!"

Theresa, or Ebony, could even come up with a quarter of a comeback to reply. All they could do was laugh. Once they had consumed half the cake and was content, Shonda motioned for the caterers to take the table away.

"I have a special gift for you," Shonda told Theresa, then dialed a number on her cellular.

Theresa couldn't hear the conversation, but it was brief. All of a sudden the music abruptly stopped. Then, *Usher's 'Nice and Sow'* began playing from the club's speakers. Now, Theresa was looking around. She just knew Usher himself was about to appear and sing her favorite song to her. That was not the case, it didn't take long for her *gift* to reveal itself. The bouncer that was standing at the entrance of the VIP booth, slowly, and seductively, approached her and began to slowly gyrate his midsection to the tempo of the song. Theresa shot a half smirk to Shonda, thinking it was pretty clever hiring a male stripper to pose as a security guard.

When the dancer ripped his shirt off, it seemed as if every female in the club including Shonda, Sheila, and Ebony were going berserk. A crowd of women had run up to the booth to get a better look. Shonda and Sheila pulled out money and were tossing bills at him. Theresa was about to pull out some bills but thought against it. It was her birthday, and this was her gift, so there was no way she was going to— he snatched his pants off, and Theresa almost fainted.

He had on the tightest briefs she'd ever seen on a man. Plus, his manhood looked like it was going to burst through the fabric. Theresa was hoping like hell it didn't, because she was so horny. There was a possible chance she would be booked for attempted rape, tonight!

As horny as Theresa was, she had to will herself not to touch him as she, her friends, and a mob of women that had entered the booth, watched him do what he was paid to do. He danced through one more song, gathered the scattered bills off the floor, then left the booth, followed by the group of women.

"Y'all some freaks!" Sheila said once the crowd left. "All of y'all need some dick!"

"We need some dick, but you're the one who was feeling on his ass!" Theresa countered.

"I was not feeling on his ass!" Sheila lied, smiling. "I made a mistake and touched it while I was stretching."

That had them all laughing hysterically.

"Y'all ready to go?" Shonda asked, looking at her watch.

"We might as well," said Ebony.

"Yeah," came Theresa. "I think we've celebrated enough."

"I gotta stop by the DJ booth and holla at Spenz," Shonda said. "Theresa, you may want to thank the crowd for showing up."

They left the VIP booth and headed for the DJ booth, where Spenz was standing in front of it with his two workers, while his protégé worked the turntables. Seeing them approach, he dismissed his workers.

"Y'all calling it a night?" he asked.

"Yep," Shonda answered. "What's the word on that?"

"He won't deal with y'all."

"He won't?" Shonda was shocked. "Why not?"

"That's what his lieutenant told me."

"That's some bullshit!" she argued. "Would you let Theresa thank the people? So, we can get the fuck outta here!"

"Yeah."

Theresa followed Spenz into the booth, where he had his surrogate DJ kill the music. Once Theresa thanked the crowd for coming out and assured them the food and drinks were still free until it was all gone, they exited the club.

"Sheila, you know you're the designated driver, right?" said Shonda.

"I wouldn't have it no other way," Sheila said, pulling out her set of keys, being that they all had a set to the truck.

As Sheila drove, Shonda pondered what Spenz had told her. She couldn't understand why L.K.S. wouldn't deal with them. Now, this left her with two choices. One, deal with L.K.S. through someone else or two, find another plug that would give them a decent deal on both products.

"Y'all might as well crash out at our spot," Shonda told Theresa and Ebony, once they made it to the highway. "I can't let y'all drive while under the influence."

"I need some birthday dick!" Theresa replied from the back seat.

"I can't tell!" said Ebony. "Spenz tried to give you some, and you turned him down. You gon' play with that coochie tonight!"

"Bullshit!" Theresa contradicted. "I know his number. As a matter of fact, as soon as we get—"

Theresa's words were cut off when their truck was struck from behind by another vehicle. Ebony and Theresa looked back, but Shonda, who was still in pain, used the right wing mirror. Behind them, was a black H-2 Hummer, occupied by two men in ball caps. The Hummer struck them again, almost causing Sheila to lose control of the Denali.

"Push it, Sheila!" Shonda yelled, holding her aching side.

Panicking, Sheila pressed the gas pedal to the floor, and the truck jerked, shooting forward. There weren't that many cars on the highway, so she didn't have to do any quick maneuvering, but to their surprise. The Hummer was keeping up, it struck again, but the blow was less severe than the first two.

"Don't give in to panic, Sheila!" Shonda prompted, seeing that her cousin was on pins and needles. "Stay focused!"

"Fuck this!" Theresa exclaimed, reaching behind the seat and snatching the tarp off the AK-47.

Theresa didn't know who these guys were, or what kind of game they were playing, but she wasn't having it. Her alcohol had worn off, and her Army trained mind had kicked in. She grabbed the assault rifle, cocked it and planted her back against the back of Shonda's seat for support. Ebony dropped her head in her lap and covered her ears as Theresa aimed the gun at the back window. Wasting no time, she squeezed off two, three-round bursts, first hitting the passenger, then the driver. The report was deafening. Now, Shonda turned around in her seat. She and Theresa watched as the Hummer veered left, crashed into the concrete median, tilt, then slam onto its right side.

"Slow it down, Sheila!" said Shonda, snapping back into her seatbelt.

"Let's just hope we don't get pulled over for that back window."

Shonda was a bit shaken up but maintained her composure. Now, she realized someone was trying to take them out of the game, *literally*!

Playa Ray

CHAPTER 17

It was almost twelve in the afternoon when Shonda forced her still-aching body out of bed. She'd thought about last night's ordeal so much, she dreamed about it, which was quite typical, being that it was a near-death experience.

Shonda didn't dwell on it for too long, because, right now, her only concern was making sure her girls were okay. She peered into Sheila's bedroom to see that she was still asleep. She then, peered into the guest room to see that Ebony and Theresa, who were sharing the same bed, were still asleep. Her next stop was the living room, where she gandered out the window. All cars were there, but her main concern was the Denali, which they had backed up to the house, in case someone saw the shattered window and dented bumper.

Now, Shonda journeyed off to the kitchen, where she washed her hands and started breakfast. In the course of doing so, Sheila showed up, taking a seat at the table. By the time Shonda was finished, Theresa and Ebony joined Sheila. Shonda didn't bother to ask either of them to set the table. She did it herself. After fixing everyone a plate and glass of orange juice, she took her seat.

"Everybody alright?" she asked, only to be regarded with grunts. "We gotta do something about the company's truck."

"We might have to take it somewhere and burn it down," Sheila replied.

"Girl, you watch way too much C.S.I.," Theresa said. "We won't have to burn it."

"We just have to get the window fixed, Sheila," said Shonda. "Ebony, since it's in your name, you'll have to be the one to take it to a body shop. I'll go with you. You up for it?"

"When?"

"Today, it's the company's truck."

"Okay," Ebony agreed. "But I wanna go home, shower, and change clothes first."

Shonda nodded. "Now, about the business. Considering what happened last night, does anybody want to back out?"

Shonda looked around the table at her girls. Neither one of them spoke. Perhaps they, too, had grown accustomed to this lifestyle and were determined not to let such scenes like last nights deter them from what they were trying to achieve. Shonda did all she could to suppress her smile. She was really awed by their perseverance.

"What body shop is open on Sunday?" Ebony asked once they finished eating.

Shonda answered, "A shop in Henry County. James took my car there, one Sunday."

Once the dishes were cleared, Shonda and Sheila walked Ebony and Theresa out to Ebony's car.

"Y'all take it easy," Shonda told them, once they were inside the car. "And watch y'all rear. If y'all feel like somebody's following y'all detour and call me."

When they'd pulled off, Shonda and Sheila retreated inside. Sheila set out to take a shower, and Shonda for reason – called Tino to fill him in on the past events that had taken place. First, she told him about the incident with Clarence, then went into last night's event.

"Damn!" Tino let out when she was done. "That was y'all?"

"You already know about that?"

"Shit, that shit was all over the news this morning!" he told her. "I do watch the news, but that shit don't sound like something y'all would do. Who the fuck y'all done pissed off?"

"This has to be some kind of drug beef," Shonda insisted. "We don't have any known enemies."

"So, what y'all gon' do?"

"We're not gonna let that shit stop us!" she promised. "As a matter of fact, we're trying to get a plug on weed and X-pills. You know anybody?"

"Not in Cali," he answered. "Every nigga I know, down South, who fuck with that stuff is shopping with that nigga L.K.S."

"He won't deal with us."

"Why not?"

"I have no idea," she answered, then wondered if he was behind these chaotic events.

172

"Send somebody else at him," Tino told her.

"I want to," she replied. "I'd rather make my own transactions, just in case a deal, somehow goes bad."

"I feel that," he stated. "Look, this is what I'm gonna do. Since y'all plan on pushing on when most niggas would've tucked their tails. I'ma send one of my lieutenants down there."

"For what?"

"To watch y'all back," he answered. "He'll get up with a few more kats in the city that don't mind bussin' their guns. Y'all are gonna need some muscle behind y'all."

"And how much is all this gonna cost?" Shonda asked, feeling as though they didn't have the money to pay for security right now.

"Don't worry about that," he told her. "He'll be down in another week."

"Is he trustworthy?"

"I trust him with my life."

****

It was the first day of July, and The Queenz had proceeded on with business, with no mishaps. Tino's lieutenant, Ant had flown down as promised and recruited three other guys to assist him with his duty, which was to accompany The Queenz on their runs. Whenever the Queenz would branch off on solo ventures, one of the guys would tag along. If they were branching off after a business run or meeting, two of them would escort Ebony and Theresa home, and two would escort Sheila and Shonda. Either way, it went, Ant would delegate himself as Shonda's personal bodyguard.

Now, Shonda was home, going over her last-minute list for the cookout that they were throwing at Grant Park, on the fourth. Seeing that everything was pretty much in order, she grabbed her cell and dialed Doolu's number. She felt she had made him wait long enough. Now, she was ready to reward him, but it was going to be on the night of the cookout. Plus, he was going to have to make that drive from Claxton.

"Yo!" Doolu answered the phone with that country southern drawl that Shonda had grown so fond of.

"What's up, Bubba?" she asked, referring to him as the name he gave all men. "What 'cha doing?"

"I guess you call me whenever them other niggas ain't acting right," Doolu said, sounding angry.

"Where did all this come from, Doolu?" she asked, knowing damn well where it was coming from, and bracing herself for the worst part.

"I'm a made nigga," he continued. "I ain't never begged a female for no pussy! Shit, I can get pussy, when I can't get a bag of weed. That's real shit!"

"Are you coming to the cookout?" she asked, hoping to ease some of the anger he had towards her.

"I got better shit to do with my time!" he spat. "As a matter of fact, make this your last time calling me!"

He hung up. Shonda looked at her phone like the battery had gone dead, instead. Doolu was a nice guy, but Shonda was looking at it as if it wasn't meant for them to hook up. Oh, well, she thought as she got off her bed and searched her closet for something to wear. Ebony and Theresa were on their way over, and they were all going to drive out to Charles' office to see if he would sell the salon to Ebony. She had already notified Ant, so he and the rest of security should already be en route. Plus, they had to make drops in East Point and College Park.

Once she'd found a pair of casual capri pants and blouse, she dressed, then went to check on Sheila.

"Sheila?" She rapped on the door that was already ajar, then pushed it open to see Sheila, who was fully dressed, standing at the vanity mirror, tending to her hair. "Did you bag those orders?"

"I did that last night," answered Sheila. "Six ounces, right?"

"Yeah."

Sheila asked, "If Charles don't sell us the salon. Can we go ahead and lease those BMWs?"

"Maybe," Shonda answered, scurrying back to her room to answer her ringing cell phone. "Yeah?"

174

"It's on y'all," Ant told her, letting her know they were outside. "We're still waiting on the other half," she replied, hanging up with him to call Theresa.

"We should be about six minutes out," Theresa answered, already knowing the reason for the call. "Just be ready."

She concluded the call, donned her heels, grabbed her pocketbook, and headed for the guest room also known as the stash room. She retrieved the orders that were already in separate paper bags marked, EP and CP. Placing them into her pocketbook, she headed for the kitchen and poured herself a cup of apple juice.

"Sheila, you want some apple juice?" she hollered out.

"I'm good," Sheila answered, rounding the corner. "You called and checked on Thelma and Louise?"

Before Shonda could answer, they heard a car's horn. Shonda finished her juice, then she and Sheila exited the house. As they neared the GMC that was driven by Ebony, Theresa dismounted and climbed into the back seat, which was her post, where she was close to the AK-47. Before climbing into the passenger seat, Shonda glanced across the street at the other Denali that was similar to theirs. The windows were heavily tinted, but she already knew that it was Ant and his allies.

"Don't forget what I said, Ebony," Shonda reminded, once she was settled in. "We can afford anything under fifteen and being that the money is coming from The Queenz Account, the profit is split four ways. It's up to you if you wanna go back to doing hair."

While Shonda and Ebony conversed, Theresa was in her own little world. Ever since that episode on the highway with the guys in the H-2 Hummer, she'd been wired up and conveying a strong urge to kill. She wouldn't dare tell this to her friend's, because she didn't want them to think the basic training she'd undergone in the Army, had turned her into a monster, even if It was true.

They finally made it to Gwinnett County. Ebony pulled the truck into the parking lot of the small, red-brick building that was Charles' office, and parked, Ant parked beside them.

"Tell them that they can stay, "Ebony started, then stopped mid-sentence when she saw Pam exit the building, followed by Charles, who playfully pinched her butt. "I'ma kill this bitch!"

Ebony reached for the door handle, but Shonda, who had also apprehended the situation, managed to reach the button on the passenger door, activating the locks.

"Let that hoodrat shit go!" Shonda told her. "You're a Queen. Queenz don't fight over men. You're supposed to be looking at the big picture. We can buy the salon and send that bitch to the unemployment line."

"That's Charles?" Theresa, who had never met Charles, asked.

"Yeah, that's the bastard!" Ebony answered.

Now, they were watching Charles and Pam, who were now standing by Pam's car, talking. After a minute or so, Pam threw her arms around his neck, and they kissed, passionately. Ebony felt like she was about to throw up. Shonda was watching Ebony. Sheila's heart went out to her friend for having to see this, which reminded her of what Andrew had done to her. Theresa was thinking of burning Charles' house down, while he was asleep!

Pam climbed into her car and pulled off as Charles headed back inside. Shonda rolled her window down and told Ant to give them a few minutes and to remain outside when they go inside.

"Let it go!" Shonda told Ebony, holding her hand. "That relationship was dead before it died. Now, it's all about business and prosperity. Success is the best revenge."

That's real!" Sheila agreed. "You just have to keep your eyes on the prize. Let karma do what it do."

"You ready?" Shonda asked.

"Let's get it done," Ebony replied, shutting off the engine, grabbing her pocketbook, and stepping out of the truck, feeling like the true Queen she was born to be.

When they entered the building, Ebony was surprised to see that the secretary was not at her desk. So, she, followed by her friends, went straight for Charles' office. The door was closed, but instead of knocking, Ebony turned the knob and entered.

"Ebony!" Charles, who was seated behind his desk, sprang to his feet. "What's going on?"

"I came to discuss business," she told him, now standing in front of his desk.

He eyed the others before asking, "What kind of business?"

"I wanna buy the salon," she answered, then realized the office had a distinctive odor, perfume!

This wasn't any ordinary perfume. This was the same exact perfume she'd smelled on his shirt from the dirty clothes hamper. The same perfume she was highly conversant with, worn by someone that she'd encountered on a regular at the salon, Pam!

"It's not for sale," Charles told her.

"I'll give you ten thousand," Ebony spoke through clenched teeth, as she fought the urge to leap across the desk and beat him senseless.

Charles' expression changed from confident to confused. "Ten thousand!"

"Yeah."

"I paid thirteen-fifty for it," he stated, folding his arms over his chest.

"Well, I'll give you thirteen-fifty," she offered.

"I don't see any profit in that."

"What would you consider a profit— fifteen?"

"Twenty."

Ebony was crushed. She remembered what Shonda said about affording anything under fifteen. Now, she was ready to walk out.

"Deal!" Shonda prompted, not liking how this was going. "We'll bring the money by, tomorrow."

"Make it two weeks," Charles said, sounding defeated.

"Two weeks it is," Shonda agreed. "Let's go ladies."

The Queenz exited the building and climbed into the GMC. As they headed for East Point to make their first drop, Shonda was thinking about the dent the twenty thousand was going to put in The Queenz Account. She knew the salon wasn't going to generate a major flow of cash, but she did it for Ebony. She knew how much

Ebony loved that shop, and how hurt she was when Charles had taken it away from her.

The drop in East Point was brief as always, which was conducted in the ladies restroom of Burger King, through the girlfriend of their client. Leaving East Point, they headed for College Park, where they were to drop off the other four ounces to two clients they did business with behind an abandoned auto parts store.

When they arrived at the drop spot, both clients were already there, still sitting in their cars. Seeing the SUVs, they immediately got out. Once security dismounted, Shonda, Sheila, and Ebony got out, leaving Theresa on her post. When the clients approached, Ebony and Sheila received their money, and Shonda handed them their order, but she noticed that Blaze, one of the clients, was cutting his eyes at their security team.

"Yeah, it's me!" Ant asserted, aggressively.

"Shit, you ain't that hard to spot," Blaze shot back.

Now, The Queenz was looking back and forth from the two, instantly sensing they knew each other and were not the best of friends. Even Theresa had heard the exchange over the truck's engine and air condition unit.

"You know that shit ain't over, right?" said Ant.

"I didn't expect it to be," Blaze replied.

What happened next, was like a scene in a western movie. They both went for their guns, but before Blaze could completely free his from the waistband of his shorts, Ant let off two shots, both slugs slamming into Blaze's skull, killing him instantly.

"Shit!" Rodney, the other client, exclaimed, before Ant fired upon him, leaving his body beside Blazes.

"Ant, what the fuck are you doing?" Shonda scolded, more concerned with the loss of two customers than the abrupt scene that just played out in front of her.

"Old beef," Ant answered, then ordered two of his men to take the cars, and the other one to search Blaze, as he did Rodney.

Two of Ant's men drove off in Blaze and Rodney's cars as he and his other man searched the bodies. While this was going on, Shonda looked around at Sheila and Ebony, surprised to see they were regarding the scene with no remorse. Somewhere in the midst of the ordeal, Theresa had dismounted the truck with the AK-47 in tow.

"Let's go, Ant!" Shonda demanded. "Right now, Queenz, get in the truck!"

Once they got what they were going to get off the bodies, Ant sent his man to the truck, then approached The Queenz.

"That was some personal shit," he told them. "I grew up in the streets. While coming up, I stepped on some nigga's toes, as well as had mine stepped on, shit happens."

At the conclusion of his speech, he headed for the truck, leaving Shonda pondering if she should inform Tino of this.

Playa Ray

CHAPTER 18

It was the Fourth of July, and the cookout The Queenz threw at Grant Park, was in full effect. DJ Spenz was doing his thing on his turntables, four catering services were hired to accommodate and people were eating, drinking, dancing, conversating and just enjoying themselves.

The Queenz were seated at a picnic table beneath a wooden awning, watching everything, while the Queenzmen which they were now known as stood guard. Although they were watching everything, Theresa mainly had her eyes on the group of women that were crowded around Spenz as he DJ'd. To say that she was jealous, would be an understatement, but she knew what she was getting into before she and Spenz had started their ongoing romance. She knew he was seeing other women. Shonda told her not to get her feelings involved. But how could she not, when she hadn't had sex in over a year, and he was capable of making her orgasm like no other man had?

"Say, Ebony?"

They all looked up to see Ted, Pam's ex-boyfriend, held at bay by one of the Queenzmen. After finding out about Charles and Pam, Ted was the last person Ebony wanted to see, although she couldn't blame him for what Pam had done.

"Can I speak with you for a minute?" he asked.

Ebony wanted to say no but remembering he was heavy in the drug game, she figured this could be a lucrative visit. Plus, they needed all the business they could get.

"Have a seat," she told him." How can I help you?"

"I'm trying to do some business with y'all," he admitted.

Being that everyone knew him, except for Theresa. Ebony introduced them before asking him what he was trying to purchase.

"Four ounces," he answered.

"We can handle that." She handed him their fake business card that could pass off as that of a private law firm. "Hit us up, and we'll make arrangements."

"I'll do that," he said, stuffing the card into his pocket. "Y'all ain't making no moves on the weed tip? I know some top buyers."

"Not yet." Shonda took the initiative. "I'll have to get at my people, this weekend."

That's exactly what Shonda intended to do. She knew one of L.K.S.'s lieutenants would be making a drop to Spenz, at the club, Saturday. She didn't have a definite plan, but she did plan on being at Club Strokers when the drop was made.

****

"Don't try nothing stupid!" Spenz asserted over the phone. "Don't even try to approach this guy!"

Shonda told Spenz she planned to try a different method with L.K.S., but withheld details. All she needed him to do was confirm that the drop was tonight which he did, but his preaching was falling on deaf ears.

"Calm down, Bishop Eddie Long!" she joked. "I don't plan on approaching anybody."

"So, how do you plan on doing it?"

"I haven't thought that far yet," she lied. "Hell, I may not even show up."

Shonda concluded the call, realizing she may have to make a subtle appearance, not only for the crowd but for Spenz, also. She didn't want to take the chance on him unintentionally blowing her cover and triggering something that didn't need to be triggered. That's when she thought about the Japanese wig she'd purchased at a convention a few years ago. Being that she was known for maintaining brown-colored hair, she knew the long, jet-black hair with its neatly-cut bang, would do the trick. Plus, she had a pair of black-framed nonmedicated glasses she would use to accommodate her look for tonight. Now, she had to find something to wear that wasn't too revealing and wouldn't draw too much attention from men.

'*A pair of baggy jeans and a plain t-shirt should work,*' she thought. As she was searching her closet for said items, she heard the ringing of the business phone.

182

"I got it!" Sheila yelled out from somewhere in the house. Moments later, she was standing in the threshold of the door that was already open. "It's Ted," she said. "He wants to know when we can drop those off to him."

Being that they didn't know too much about Ted, or what kind of stunt he might try to pull, Shonda took it upon herself to methodize the transaction. Once it was confirmed that it would be made at his home in Gwinnett, and he would be the only person present, Shonda assured him the drop would be tomorrow.

"What, you got a date?" Sheila asked when Shonda hung up.

"Why'd you ask?"

"Because you were pulling out clothes when I came to your room."

"Black people are so nosey!" Shonda asserted, heading for her room, with Sheila at her heels. "I have a date, but not like what you think. It's pretty much a business date."

"Hell, I need some kind of date!" Sheila confessed when they returned to Shonda's room. I ought to have cobweb between my legs by now."

"That's a good thing."

"How's that?"

"It shows that you're more in control of who you have sex with," Shonda explained. "Your standards are much higher now. You refuse to eat chicken when you can have steak. That's some real, Queen shit! Queenz don't settle for less."

Sheila knew everything Shonda said was true, because, as bad, as she was in need to be touched by a man. She just couldn't seem to allow just *any* man into her palace. No matter how fine she thought they were. For some reason, she started thinking about, Ray. She wished he was still alive because he was more than worthy, not only to enter her palace but to lay claim to it and rule over it however he wanted to.

****

Shonda pulled her Mustang into the parking lot of Club Strokers and parked. Before dismounting, she gave herself a once over in the rearview mirror and giggled at what Sheila had said about her going out as *Jane Bond*, with the Japanese wig and librarian glasses.

Shonda got out and approached the building, almost forgetting she had to wait in a line full of men that were regarding her with awkward looks, but neither of them attempted to strike up a conversation with her, in which she was thankful for. Perhaps they figured she was here for the same reason as they were.

She thought that it would take forever, but she only stood in line for about seven minutes. When she entered the club, she looked towards the DJ booth to see Spenz working the turntables. Only one of his workers was standing nearby. Before finding a table, Shonda headed for the bar, passing Clyde, the owner, who regarded her the same as the guys outside the club had. He didn't recognize her, which was good. After ordering a cup of Grey Goose, she found an unoccupied table and sat facing the DJ booth, so she could see the transaction when it happens.

As she sparsely sipped her drink, she surveyed the club. The only times she'd been here was on Theresa's birthday, and the New Year Eve's party that The Kingz had thrown, which was the night they'd met. Now, being here on a regular night, she was amazed by how relaxed the atmosphere was. The music was pumping, the dancers were performing their usual erotic routines, but the men just mechanically sipped their beverages as they tipped the dancers for their services.

"Lap dance, or table dance?"

Shonda looked up at the dancer that had posed the question. It was the light-skin blonde that seemed to be quite interested in them at the birthday party, last week. To be honest, she had been waiting on a dancer to proposition her, so she wouldn't look too conspicuous sitting alone, but she didn't expect to be approached by this one.

'*Fuck it!*' she thought. "Lap dance," she finally answered, pulling out the wad of bills that she brought for this purpose.

The blonde didn't waver. She, in her blue G-string and matching top, stood in front of Shonda and began grinding to the music.

Shonda noted that the woman, who was her complexion was pretty much her same height. The dancer turned around and made her ass clap, before straddling Shonda in a reverse cowgirl position, and grinding on her lap. In lieu of planting bills in her G-string, Shonda used the table beside her.

Shonda was so caught up in watching the dancer, she'd almost forgot her purpose for being there. She looked up and spotted a guy approaching the DJ booth. He was short, stocky, and wore his hair pulled back into a ponytail. He fit the description of one of L.K.S.'s lieutenants, as told to her by Spenz. He entered the booth as Spenz went into another song. They dapped and made small talk. Their transaction was subtle, but not to Shonda because she was well aware of what was taking place.

"So, which King were *you* messing with?"

Shonda was so busy watching the booth, she hadn't noticed the dancer had changed positions and was now sitting in her lap, facing her, no longer dancing, but what surprised her was the fact that the stripper recognized her.

"If you're tired, I can find someone else," Shonda said, pretending like she hadn't heard the question.

"I'm not moving until you answer my question," the blonde stated. "Don't take this as a threat, but my fight game is superb. All I want is an answer."

Shonda locked eyes with her, of course, she took that shit as a threat! Now, she was considering pushing this bitch to the floor and branding Nike signs all over her face, but she had other things going on tonight.

"King James," Shonda answered. "Now get off me before I get curious about that superb fight game of yours!"

The blonde obediently got up and walked away, leaving her tips on the table, but Shonda didn't look after her. Instead, she looked towards the booth to see Ponytail heading for the exit. Leaving the rest of the bills on the table, she casually got up and strolled towards the door, eyeing the booth from the corner of her eyes. Spenz wasn't paying her any attention.

When she'd made it outside, she saw her target getting into the passenger side of a white Lexus on chrome wheels. The engine immediately came alive, and the driver pulled out. This made Shonda quick step to her car. By the time she'd slid behind the wheel, the Lexus was leaving the parking lot. When she'd made it to the exit, she saw that the Lexus was slowly making its way down Brocket Road, possibly headed for the expressway.

Shonda pulled her Ford out into the light traffic and followed at a distance she felt suitable. As she kept them in sight, she thought about the blonde stripper, wondering why it was significant for her to know which King Shonda used to date. Now, it was clear to Shonda that she may have had ties to one of The Kingz, but the big question was, which one?

Shonda noticed that the Lexus had turned down a residential street. She initiated her right turn signal, and accelerated a little, hoping to catch them before they pull into a garage if that was the case. She made the turn, hoping to see their tail lights, but didn't. Therefore, she gunned the engine a little, but she didn't get too far when she came upon the Lexus that was parked in the middle of the street with the lights off. Before she could come to a complete stop, the driver and passenger, both lunged from the car, and surrounded her car on both sides, carrying handguns. That's when Shonda realized she may have committed suicide.

CHAPTER 19

"You must be lost, yo?" the driver, who approached the driver side, asserted in an up North accent.

Instantly, Shonda knew from Spenz' description that this was L.K.S.'s other lieutenant, who was a member of the Bloods gang. Plus, the red bandanna around his neck was confirmation.

"Not really," Shonda answered, which was all she could come up with.

"So, you don't think we know you were following us?" he asked. "You wanna tell us why?"

She couldn't seem to fabricate a lie, so she told the truth. "I wanna meet with L.K.S. and find out why he won't deal with The Queenz."

"So, Spenz didn't tell y'all why?"

"Spenz told us that L.K.S. won't deal with us."

"He didn't tell y'all why?"

"I guess not," Shonda cast a glance at Ponytail, who was standing on the passenger side, basically looking around.

"He said he won't deal with false claimers," Red Bandanna let out.

"False claimers!"

"Y'all are getting fame off The Kingz' names," he explained. "Plus, neither of the Kingz was married, so there couldn't possibly be any *Kingz Widows* running around."

"We've never claimed to be The Kingz' widows!" Shonda took offense. "L.K.S. don't know shit! If he's a close friend of theirs, then he would know that I was dating James before he died."

"He was *real* close to them," he replied as if he'd also taken offense, "But he don't remember you."

Shonda's mind automatically started to work. She was trying to remember all of James' associates, and see whose name would benefit the initials L.K.S.

"Put your car in reverse!" Red Bandanna interrupted her thoughts.

"Huh?"

"Put your car in reverse!" he repeated. "Back all the way back to the main road and find you something safe to do. Next time, I won't be this nice."

Thankful for the pass, Shonda did what she was told. Now, as she drove home, she had two things on her mind. The dancer and L.K.S., who were both linked to The Kingz, somehow. Remembering that Spenz had told her that L.K.S. had contacted him, and he not telling her everything L.K.S. said, she wondered if he actually knew the guy, and was withholding his identity at L.K.S.' request.

****

"Get the door, Ebony!" Theresa yelled from the bathroom, where she was applying eyeliner.

She knew it was Spenz. They had made plans to have lunch, catch a movie at the Magic Johnson Theater, and come back to the house for a little cuddling before it was time to head to Gwinnett.

"It's Spenz," Ebony yelled back to her.

"Tell him I'll be right out."

Finishing with her cosmetics, Theresa, who was already dressed in a pair of blue jeans capri pants, red tank top, and open-toed heels, headed for her bedroom, where she grabbed her pocketbook making sure her registered gun was in it. Then entered the living room, where Ebony and Spenz were standing around, talking.

"There's my Queen!" Spenz asserted. "You look stunning!"

"Thank you!" She kissed him, then turned to Ebony. "Have y'all decided where y'all are having lunch?"

"Not that I know of," Ebony answered. "I left that up to my mom, but I won't know until I pick them up."

"Will you be alright without security?"

"I should."

"Just make sure you take that with you!"

"I am."

"Okay, I'll see you later."

They hugged, then Theresa and Spenz exited. When they got to his green Chevy Tahoe, he made sure to open the door for her and help her in before climbing behind the wheel.

"I told you about the DJ battle that's coming up in September, right?" Spenz asked as he drove.

"You did," she answered, feeling as though he was about to ask her to accompany him to the event.

"Well, right after I got off the phone with you," he started. "I got a call from the host. He said they haven't picked any judges yet and wanted me to ask if The Queenz would do the honors."

Theresa was immediately hit with déjà vu. The last time the Battle of The DJs was held, was two years ago when The Kingz signed on as judges but were murdered en route to the event.

Theresa remembered being there with Sheila, Shonda, and Ebony when the club owner announced the heart-breaking news to the crowd. It really crushed her, because she was really feeling Fred, and enjoyed hanging out with the rest of The Kingz. It was rumored that the event didn't take place last year, because of what happened to them.

"I thought the battle was usually held in August," she now replied, remembering that The Kingz died in August 2003.

"It is," he answered. "This year, they were a lil slow at putting things together, so they pushed it to September to give themselves more time."

"And they want us to judge?"

"That's what they're asking."

"I'll have to talk to the girls about it," she told him, wondering if they would feel the same way she felt about it.

****

Ebony had picked up Erica and her mother at her mother's house and driven out to the Spaghetti Factory, which was where her mother had always wanted to go.

"You haven't decided on what kind of dessert you want?" Ebony asked her mother, who was seated beside her.

"I was thinking about that double-chocolate cake," she answered, still trying to finish her chicken pasta salad.

"Well, you need to be trying to save some room for it!" Erica, who was seated across from them, advised. "Once that pasta blows up inside you, the only thing you'll be thinking about is making it to the toilet."

"Don't worry about my digestive system!" Ms. Davis countered. "You need to start eating and stop starving yourself for that nappy head boyfriend of yours!"

"I'm on a diet, mama," Erica replied. "And I'm not doing it for him. I'm doing what my personal trainer advised me to do."

"Personal trainer?" Ebony asked.

"I told you I was in the gym."

"You told me that you were *thinking* about going to the gym."

"Well, I'm going to a gym in Buckhead," Erica admitted. "I just wanna eat healthy and stay in shape. Y'all should join me. It ain't like y'all got jobs."

"And speaking of jobs," their mother interjected, "Ebony, how are you able to get by without one? Erica has a sugar daddy. You got one, too?"

"I still have money in my account from the salon," Ebony answered, not wanting to lie to her mother, and definitely not wanting to reveal to them that she was a drug dealer. She was surprised she had kept it away from Erica this far, although she was always with her mysterious boyfriend, who no one had yet to meet. Ebony was beginning to believe she was keeping him secret for a reason.

****

"What's new?" Tino answered his phone.

Shonda and Sheila had just made it back to the house, after dropping their grandmother off at home. Being that they hadn't spent time with her in a while, they decided to take her out to eat, and grocery shopping.

"I need your help," Shonda told Tino as she flopped down on her bed.

He sighed. "I'm listening."

"I'm trying to expand," she explained. "But it seems like I can't make the right connections. The money ain't coming in like it's supposed to."

"Don't let 'cha eyes get bigger than ya' stomach!" he told her. "Y'all are trying to follow in The Kingz footsteps and do what they did, but it's not gonna happen."

Shonda took offense. "Why, because we're women?"

"Nope, because y'all ain't prepared to do what they did to get where they were and accomplish what they accomplished."

"Which is?"

"Rob and kill big time drug dealers."

Shonda was taken aback by his answer. She knew The Kingz were capable of such things, but she didn't think they had actually executed them. Hell, she'd heard rumors of them holding court for people that violated them and mutilated their bodies as a means of prosecution.

'*But it was all rumors*,' she thought. "Do you know that for sure?" Shonda asked. "You can't believe—"

"Everybody knew this," he cut her off. "Niggas don't accumulate as much dope and money as they did, in two years. I know niggas that's been in the game, damn near ten years, and ain't got *half* the shit them niggas had."

"You gonna help me, or not?" Shonda asked, ready to change the subject.

"You still haven't told me what you need."

"I need you to front me some bricks."

"Shit, I ain't got it like that!" he told her. "But there's a dude down your way, Vincent. He's a loan shark for drug dealers. If you want me to, I'll set an appointment for y'all."

"Can I trust him?"

"He does good business," said Tino. "Whatever deal y'all make with him, make sure y'all stay true to it. I shouldn't have to tell you what'll happen if y'all don't."

"Make the call."

Getting off the phone with Tino, Shonda traded her heels for a pair of sneakers and headed for the kitchen, where Sheila had Ted's order on the table and was talking on her cell phone. Hanging up, she informed Shonda that the Queenzmen were already outside, and Ebony and Thresa were ready to be picked up. After re-checking the order, they were out the door, and on their way to Riverdale.

"I wanna call a brief Queenz meeting, if I may," said Theresa, as soon as she'd climbed into the truck.

"We're all here," said Shonda, who was driving.

"I was out with Spenz today," she started. "He told me that the host of the Battle of The DJs called him and wanted him to ask if the Queenz would do the honors of judging the event."

Everyone was quiet. The only thing that could be heard was the radio playing *Gucci Mane's 'So Icy.'*

"I think we should do it," Shonda finally said.

"I wouldn't mind," said Ebony.

"What!" Sheila opposed. "Don't forget what happened to—"

"We're not forgetting what happened to them," Shonda cut in. "Besides, what happened to them, didn't happen *at* the event. I've thought about that, over a million times. They had a lot of enemies. Their appearance at the event was internationally known. I assume that's how one of their enemies was able to get the drop on them. Now, I won't lie and say we don't have enemies, because that's part of being in the game. Hell, we may even have a few of The Kingz' enemies, but that shouldn't stop us from showing up at certain events. We just have to learn from their mistakes. If we go, it can't be broadcasted. Only if we all decide to go. Anybody don't wanna go?"

When no one answered, Shonda told Theresa to let Spenz know that they would do it, and if it was broadcasted that they would be there, then they'd pull out. Getting to Ted's house, Shonda chose to park in front of the house, instead of the driveway, just in case things got out of hand, and they had to get out of there with the quickness. The Queenz dismounted and approached the house, followed by the Queenzmen, who had parked behind them.

Clearly, Ted had seen them pull up because he had the door open before they could reach the porch, allowing them in. He'd even took the initiative to let the Queenzmen search the house for any other occupants.

"Shall we do this?" Ted asked, taking a seat on the living room sofa, across from the coffee table that contained a scale and two stacks of bills. After receiving the product from Sheila, Shonda joined him on the sofa.

While they were conducting business, Ebony's mind was full of evil thoughts. She could not help but think about Charles and Pam as she attentively watched Ted. Now, she was thinking about calling Ted later, seducing him into sex, parading him around, and having him accompany her to the salon when she went to inform the staff that she was the new owner, knowing that would give Pam a double slap in the face.

The sound of the doorbell pulled her from her reverie and had everybody looking at Ted, who seemed just as inquisitive as they were.

"You expecting company?" Ant asked.

"Hell no!" Ted answered, getting off the sofa and approaching the door, where he looked through the peephole before opening the door wide enough to speak to his unwanted guest. "What did I tell you about showing up without calling?"

"You got company?" It was a feminine voice.

"I'm trying to handle some business."

"Well, I came over to chill with you," she said. "You want me to wait on the porch until you're done?"

Ted dropped his head like he was trying to figure out what to do with her. Then he asked, "If I let you in, will you wait in the bedroom?"

"I can do that?"

Ted let her in. When she entered, Shonda slowly rose to her feet, conveying the same puzzled look as the other Queenz. Out of all the people in the world, they would have never expected to encounter her here.

Playa Ray

CHAPTER 20

Leaving Ted's house, Shonda dropped Theresa and Ebony off at their home, and she and Sheila returned to their home, where they ate dinner, and watched TV until Sheila journeyed off to take her shower and prepare for bed.

Shonda didn't tell Sheila that she was going out tonight, so as soon as she felt Sheila was sound asleep, she was out the door. It was almost one o'clock, and she knew, on Sundays, Club Strokers would usually close at two. She just hoped that Spenz didn't exit the building before the blonde dancer did, being that he was highly familiar with her car.

When she pulled into the parking lot, it was twenty-three minutes after one. She made sure to park at the end of the lot with the rear of her car facing the club, thankful for the tinted windows. As she sat, watching the club through the rear window, she couldn't help but think about encountering Erica at Ted's house, earlier. At first, she thought Ebony and Erica were going to lunge into a shouting match, but Erica surprised them all, when she headed for Ted's bedroom before, disregarding them like she'd never seen either one of them a day in her life. It didn't dawn on Shonda, until later, that what Erica did, was probably the best thing to do. She also realized that Erica probably didn't mention to Ted that she was Ebony's sister.

Of course, Ted would have mentioned that to Ebony. Now, Shonda noticed men were starting to exit the club. She watched as the parking lot became almost empty. When there was no more movement for a while, she figured the rest of the vehicles belonged to the club's staff. Then, to her surprise, the blonde exited the club, but she was accompanied by Spenz. Shonda just hoped he didn't spot her car. She also hoped he didn't plan on following the blonde home for a little roll in the hay, because that would jeopardize her mission. As she watched them approach a red BMW convertible, where they stood and chatted, she couldn't help but believe they were close friends of L.K.S.', who claimed to be close friends of The Kingz. He contacted Spenz, who used to work for both, Ray and James, and offered to be his supplier. Then, the dancer seemed to be hell-bent on finding out which King Shonda was involved with. So, there was no doubt in Shonda's mind that these two were mutually in cahoots with L.K.S.

Still watching the scene, Shonda saw Clyde come to the door, say something to one of them, then duck back inside. Seconds later, Spenz gave the dancer a friendly hug, then headed for the building. Shonda couldn't have been more relieved. She waited until the dancer pulled her BMW out of the parking lot before starting her car and following her, hoping she was not as cautious as L.K.S.'s lieutenants were.

Everything seemed to be going well as Shonda trailed her car along the expressway, at about forty yards back. She closed the gap a little when the BMW got off on Sylvan Road exit and maintained a good distance as they rode down Sylvan Road. Then, the BMW turned on Burns Drive and seemed to speed up. When Shonda made the turn, there was no sign of the car. This made her slow down, feeling like she was coming upon an ambush. Then, in front of a white house, she saw the blonde step out onto the sidewalk with her pocketbook over her shoulder and her hands on her hips. Getting closer, she saw the BMW in the driveway.

Clearly, the dancer had spotted Shonda and was waiting for her. So, seeing no need of trying to play it off, Shonda stopped in front of her.

"You can't park in the middle of the street," she told Shonda before turning and heading for the front door.

It didn't take a rocket scientist to tell Shonda that she had been invited in. Not feeling a bad vibe about this, Shonda pulled her car into the driveway, behind the BMW. By the time she got out, the dancer had already entered the house, leaving the door open. Entering, Shonda was stunned by the layout of the living room, from the all-white leather furniture to the ostrich feathered rug. Even the large, built-in-wall aquarium with the sundry exotic-looking fish, seemed too expensive for the income of an exotic dancer.

'*This stuff has L.K.S. written all over it,*' Shonda thought.

"You suck at being a private eye!" the blonde asserted upon entering the living room carrying a bottle of Moet and two wine glasses, placing them on the table. "I spotted your car in the parking lot, as soon as I came out of the club. I know what everybody at the club drives. Neither one of them drives a black Mustang."

"So, how did you know I was following you?" Shonda asked.

"I saw you pull out the parking lot."

"How'd you know it was me?"

"Close the door and have a seat!" she said, taking a seat in the chair, pouring Moet in both glasses.

Shonda closed the door and took a seat on the sofa, close to the chair.

"You were following me for a reason." She handed Shonda one of the glasses. "Why?"

"I have a few questions to ask you," Shonda answered, sipping her drink.

"I'm listening."

"Which King did you have ties to?" Shonda plunged in as formal as she could.

"Black," she answered, sipping her drink. "He's my son's father."

"Felicia!" Shonda blurted out, now remembering that James had told her about Black's baby mama who was a stripper.

Felicia nodded.

"Well, I'm Shonda." She held her hand out.

"I know," Felicia shook her hand.

"So, who is L.K.S.?" Shonda ventured.

"A close friend of The Kingz."

"You know him?"

"Not that I know of," answered Felicia. "He sends me money for Kevin, through Spenz, that's it."

Shonda couldn't tell if she was lying, but the moment she'd mentioned Black's name, her eyes constantly blinked as if she was trying to blink back her tears and maintain her composure. For that reason, Shonda chose not to pry any further.

"So, how's Kevin?"

****

Ebony was anticipating Erica's arrival. She was so anxious, she'd been pacing the living room floor for the past thirty minutes, ever since Erica had called from Ted's house saying that they needed to talk. Ebony was really anticipating this because she couldn't believe Erica had gone behind her back and did what she told her not to do.

Ebony heard loud music coming from outside and went to the window to see Ted's Cadillac Escalade pull into the driveway, parking behind Ebony's car, being that Theresa wasn't there. She had driven out to Spenz' place. Ebony rushed to the door, opened it, and stood akimbo as Erica approached.

"I'm finna' get on your ass!" Ebony voiced. "Come on in here!"

"Don't start no shit, it won't be no shit!" Erica replied as she entered, and Ebony closed the door. She took a seat on the sofa.

"Why you ain't tell me you were messing with, Ted?" Ebony asked, now standing on the other side of the coffee table, across from Erica.

"Probably the same reason why you ain't tell me you were a big-time drug dealer," Erica responded. "And I still have a hard time believing that shit."

"Did you tell him that you're my—"

"Hell no!" Erica exclaimed. "If I did, he would probably get paranoid, thinking I'd set him up for y'all to rob him. I'd rather keep it like it is."

****

It had been two weeks since The Queenz agreed to meet with Charles about the salon, so they, followed by the Queenzmen, were on their way to his office to close the deal.

"Hello?" Shonda, who was in the back seat, answered her cell phone.

"Attorney Mathew Shields," the lawyer announced. "Is this, Ms. Shonda Watson?"

"It is."

"I have good news!"

"I'm listening."

"The Captain who you allegedly assaulted—" he began, "—has dropped the charge against you."

"What about the lieutenant?" Shonda asked, already knowing the answer.

"Hers is still pending."

"What about a court date?"

"I haven't heard anything yet."

"So, with one charge dropped," Shonda ventured. "Does your fee go down?"

"Twenty-five is what I charge for *one* assault," he told her. "I was just doing that on the strength of—"

"Yeah, yeah," she cut in. "Just make sure I don't go to prison!"

When they'd entered Charles' office, he seemed as though he was ready to do business, greeting them with a smile while shaking their hands.

"Have a seat, ladies!" he told them, then settled in behind his desk.

The Queenz all sat in the four chairs he had lined up for them. Ebony, who was carrying the briefcase with the twenty thousand dollars in it, placed it atop his desk.

"Where's the deed?" she asked.

"Right here." He handed over the documents.

"You can go ahead and count the money," Shonda told him, knowing Ebony wanted to stop by the salon before they headed for Bankhead Highway, where they had to make a drop.

"I'll go with my instincts on this one," he told her. "I'll count it later."

"Y'all wanna read this?" Ebony asked, holding the deed out.

Shonda asked, "Did you read it?"

"Yeah."

"Is it decent?"

"Yeah."

"Sign it."

Ebony signed the papers and they left, heading for the salon. Ebony couldn't wait to see the look on Pam's face when she announced to everyone that there was a *new sheriff* in town,' but Ebony was highly disappointed when they arrived and was informed by Khandi that Pam who was the manager, by the way, had quit last week. Now, Ebony was guessing that was the reason Charles wanted two weeks. To convince Pam to quit.

After Ebony shared the news with the stylists and appointed Khandi as manager, The Queenz left for Atlanta to see Montez, who had moved from Harris Homes, and now resided on Bankhead Highway. Ebony turned the truck onto Cedar Avenue and parked in front of the house that Montez had described to them. Dismounting, they, followed by the Queenzmen, approached the front door. Ebony knocked, moments later, Montez opened the door, letting them in. There was another guy sitting on the living room sofa, who was highly familiar to Shonda and Sheila.

"What's up, Bankhead!" Shonda greeted with a smile.

"Oh, shit!" he exclaimed, not getting up. "I know y'all ain't The Queenz!"

"Yep," she answered. "You still trafficking?"

"Shit, I stay getting to the money!" he bragged. "What's up, Griffin?"

"I can't call it, Bankhead," Sheila answered. "How you doing?"

"I'm good, but my name ain't, Bankhead, it's Dee."

"Okay, Dee," Sheila asserted, smiling.

"Shit, I'm out now, Shawty," he told Shonda.

"I see that." Shonda knew where this was going.

"I'm still trying to get at you," he admitted. "At least, let me take you out. It ain't like I'm a broke nigga!"

"Not right now, Dee," Shonda replied. "I got too much on my plate at the moment. Maybe some other time."

"That's what's up."

Concluding the deal with Montez, they were back in the truck, and heading back up Cedar Avenue, approaching Bankhead.

"Shonda, there go, Mario!" Sheila, who was seated in the front passenger seat, said.

Shonda, who had just looked down at her vibrating cell phone to see Tino's number, jerked her head up, and couldn't believe what she was seeing. Mario, who was clad in a pair of dingy jeans, dirty white shoes and shirt, was walking down Bankhead with some female that basically looked like she'd been sleeping under a bridge. As soon as Ebony stopped the truck, Shonda, disregarded Tino's call, lunged from the back seat, and approached Mario with the zeal of a lioness, stopping them both in their tracks.

"Give me one reason why I shouldn't break this phone across your fuckin' head!" Shonda snapped.

Mario, who was in dire need of a shave, haircut, and shower, stumbled backward, looking as if he was trying to remember her. "Hey, baby!" he said, revealing a missing tooth. "I came by the house. You don't even stay there no more. Then you changed your number."

"Mario, you don't have no reason to look for me!" Shonda asserted, noticing that her girls were now standing beside her.

"I was trying to get something I left in your closet."

Shonda had almost forgotten about the kilo he'd left on the day he'd stolen her car. The same kilo that had got The Queenz where they are now. Although Shonda felt, in the beginning, that the kilo belonged to her for what he'd put her through, she knew, deep down inside, it still belonged to him. Or whoever he'd taken it from.

"I found that," she told him.

"You did!" His eyes were the size of saucers.

She was about to hand him one of her cards, but thought against it, because it appeared as though he wasn't aware of their fame and success. Therefore, she jotted down her cell phone number and handed it to him. That's when she noticed how small he'd gotten, but the small needle-size punctures in the fold of his arms is what stood out the most.

"Call me," she told him. "I'll make sure you get it back."

When they returned to the truck, all Shonda could do was shake her head as she watched Mario and his cavewoman continue down

Bankhead, perhaps in search of their next high. Then, immediately, she thought about Tino, whose call she had ignored. She knew he wouldn't call unless it was about business. Therefore, she had to call him back.

"I just called your high-yellow ass a few minutes ago!" Tino said through the phone.

"I know," she replied. "I was tending to some business. What's up?"

"Y'all got a meeting with Vincent, tomorrow," he told her. "I told him y'all were looking for at least ten birds and a whole bell of marijuana."

"That's good enough."

****

The next day, The Queenz pulled into the parking lot of the building Tino gave them the address to. The lot was half-packed with vehicles, and there were people moving to and fro, clad in suits and ties, hence the reason why Tino probably told them to dress for business.

When they entered the place, they headed for the elevators as they were instructed, passing more casually dressed people, who were probably insurance agents, being that the sign out front read: *Worldwide Insurance Agency.*

Getting to the sixth floor which was on the top floor. The Queenz stepped off the elevator and were met by four, well-dressed men, who lightly frisked them, then led them to a pair of double-doors. One of the guys pushed the doors open and stepped aside to let them enter the large room, where it was, at least, twenty-five yards to the desk where a rather large man was seated.

"The Queenz!" Vincent stood, shaking their hands. "It's nice to finally get to meet y'all. Please, have a seat."

They sat in the four visitor's chairs as he retook his seat.

"I was wondering if I would ever get to do business with y'all," he continued. Then, to Shonda, he said, "I've dealt with your late boyfriend, the legendary King James!"

So, that's how James was able to pull off his side hustle, Shonda reflected. Vincent was probably the source behind their quick rise to success. So, there was no doubt in her mind that they were on their way to the big leagues.

Playa Ray

CHAPTER 21

Shonda couldn't believe how fast their pounds of weed was going. It seemed that people were waiting for them to find a plug, so they could shop with them for the same reason others shopped with them on the cocaine. They were The Kingz' widows.

The night of the DJ battle was finally here, and The Queenz were all assembled at Theresa and Ebony's house, waiting for the stretch Cadillac truck Ebony had ordered to take them to the event. Plus, they'd all decided to wear skirts and open toe heels with their diamond-encrusted tiaras, and assorted jewelry.

"Girl, for you to have no ass, you look good in that skirt!" Sheila told Theresa when Theresa entered the living room, where they were seated.

"You gon' get off my ass!" Theresa stated, taking a seat on the sofa between Sheila and Shonda.

"I can't get off something you don't have!" Sheila shot back.

"Y'all crazy!" Shonda said, laughing. "I don't know why, but I feel like smoking a blunt."

Now, everyone was looking at Shonda. They knew she had re-nounced that habit the night The Kingz died. Ebony had quit when she met Charles, and Theresa hadn't mentioned anything about smoking, ever since she returned from South Carolina. Sheila had never tried the stuff.

"I feel like you deserve one," Sheila finally said, "Hell, I'ma get my drink on tonight! As a matter of fact, if you fire up a blunt, pass it my way!"

Now, everyone was regarding Sheila. They just knew she was joking, although her expression said otherwise.

"Anybody else wanna get their lungs out of pawn?" Shonda asked once she saw that Sheila was serious.

"Hell yeah!" Ebony answered.

Theresa said, "Might as well."

"My girls!" Shonda prompted, pulling an already rolled blunt from her purse.

"Ooh wee, heifer!" Sheila exclaimed. "You already had one rolled!"

"Just in case," Shonda lit the blunt, taking a long drag.

By the time they were halfway done with the blunt, they heard the sound of a car's horn, indicating that the limousine had arrived. Shonda called Ant, who was already outside with the others and told him to let the limousine driver know they'd be out in five minutes. Although it took ten minutes to finish the blunt and freshen their breaths from the smell of the weed. When they exited the house, the driver was already standing by the white stretch Escalade.

"Hello, Ms. Davis!" he greeted Ebony, as he opened the door for them.

"Hey!" Ebony spoke, not able to recall his name, or if he'd ever told her what it was.

"I'm more than happy to be at your service again," he said.

"And I'm more than happy to have you again," Ebony replied, and climbed into the truck.

"Girl, what you got going on with the limo driver?" Shonda asked once they were all settled in.

"That's the one I had dinner with on Charles' birthday," answered Ebony.

"Oh, that's him?" asked Sheila. "He's too fine to be a limo driver!"

"What's his name?" Theresa wanted to know.

"Um—" Ebony tried again, to no avail. She knew the only way to find out was to ask. She pressed the button that lowered the privacy glass. "Driver?"

"Yes?"

"You never told me your name."

"Phillip," he answered.

"And what's the odds of you being my driver again?" she asked, making small talk.

Well, once again, I'm filling in for another sick driver."

"So, whenever a driver is out, you're the one that has to step in?"

"Well, I own the company," he answered. "And I feel that I'm obligated to step in, in order to satisfy my customers and keep my business going."

'*Own the company?*' Ebony thought. After conforming to Queenz status, she had pretty much raised her standards when it came to men, and right now, Phillip seemed to be an object of her desire. Therefore, she jotted her number down and handed it to him when they arrived at The Warehouse, where the event was being held.

Once the Queenzmen joined them, The Queenz headed for the entrance, passing the people that were regarding them with interest. They didn't expect The Queens to show up, because the radio broadcasting of the event asserted the event would be judged by a panel of special surprise guests.

"Hello, ladies!" The club's owner met them at the entrance. "Thanks for coming out. Allow me to escort you all to the judges' panel!"

They followed him to the VIP booth, looking around at the crowd and the DJs that were crowded around the two DJ stations they were going to actuate for the battle. Theresa was looking for Spenz in the small crowd but couldn't see him. When they got to the booth and had taken their seats, the owner left, promising to send their drinks up.

"You see your husband?" Shonda asked Theresa when she spotted Spenz.

"I do now."

"Did you tell him that we're gonna let the crowd judge?"

"Nope."

"Here are y'all drinks."

Two, well-dressed females entered the booth with two bottles of Cognac on ice, and plastic cups. When they left, The Queenz even Sheila wasted no time pouring themselves a cup of the cold beverage.

"Ladies and gentlemen!" the host sounded over the loudspeakers. "I'm your host, Gold Mouth, and I'd like to welcome you all to the two thousand five, Battle of the DJs. Tonight, our panel consists of four, lovely, and extremely beautiful women. Y'all give it up for The Queenz.

The Queenz stood as the crowd erupted with cheers and applause.

"Now," Gold Mouth continued, once the crowd had settled. "We have a mighty large lineup tonight. I mean under this very roof, we got DJ Envy, DJ Rock, DJ Red Alert, DJ Spenz, DJ Diamond Kutz, DJ Snake, DJ Goldfinger, DJ K. Steel, DJ Shane, DJ Drama, DJ Mike Fresh, DJ Yeah, DJ Fat Boi, DJ Flyy, DJ Cyclone, DJ Rolex, DJ Foxxy Lady, DJ Skully, DJ Taliban and DJ Ruck Sack. All of these DJs have traveled from various parts of the world to prove their skills on the wheels of steel. Now, I wanna recognize DJ Goldfinger for his two, consecutive wins. If he wins tonight, he will be crowned: *Master of the Mix*, and go into the DJs Hall of Fame. Now, without further ado, let's do this shit like it's 'pose to be did!'"

Gold Mouth called the first two DJs up, and the battle was in full effect. Spenz was in the fourth round, defeating DJ Shane, who had defeated the first three DJs, based on the cheers from the crowd. Two more bottles of Cognac and a 2-liter bottle of Sprite were brought up to The Queenz, who had more cups brought up for the Queenzmen.

While sipping from her cup and enjoying the show, a group of guys entering the club caught Sheila's attention. There were five of them, but the well-dressed one in the dark suit and matching brasilin was the one that sparked her interest. There was something about the way the other four guys stuck close to him as if they were his bodyguards. She watched as they found a spot along the back wall, with he and two of his guys leaning against it, and the other two standing in front of them. Sheila couldn't see the man's face for the brim of the hat, but her eyes were automatically stuck on him. Then, as soon as she tilted her cup to take another swill, the guy looked up at the booth, causing her to choke, and spit her drink back out.

"Girl, you okay?" Theresa asked, patting her on the back.

Sheila didn't answer, instead, she looked back at the man, who diverted his attention to the battle, with the brim hiding his face again, but she didn't have to see it again to confirm what she'd seen.

She wasn't even going to trick herself into blaming the weed and alcohol, she'd seen his face!

Putting her cup down, Sheila abruptly got up and marched out of the booth. She descended the steps as fast as her heels would allow her and pushed through the crowd unaware that Shelton, her bodyguard, was right behind her. When she cleared the crowd, she saw that his men had formed a fortress around him to block her off, as if they were expecting her. Stopping in her tracks, she looked past them to see that he had his head down, which gave her more confirmation. If it wasn't him, then why was he hiding his face?

This left her no choice but to call out his name. "*Ray!*"

Playa Ray

CHAPTER 22

"Sheila, wake your drunk hallucinating ass up!"

Sheila roused from her sleep to see Shonda standing over her. Fighting her hangover, she was not in the mood to be bantered by Shonda about who she'd seen last night. She knew she had seen Ray, but by the time she'd made it back to the booth to tell the others, he and his men had exited the building, because she couldn't spot either one of them in the crowd, which had the other Queenz under the impression that she was already intoxicated, but Sheila knew she wasn't drunk, or hallucinating. She saw who she saw!

"What?" Sheila whined, holding her head that felt as though it weighed a ton.

"It's after eleven," Shonda told her. "The Queenz Distribution is in full effect, today. We got money to make. Breakfast should be ready in two minutes."

Shonda, who was already dressed, left the room, heading back to the kitchen to check on the last of the bacon she had been frying. As she poured grits into the already-boiling water, her cell phone vibrated on her hip. The number indicated that the call was coming from a pay phone.

"Hello?"

"Shonda?" Mario asked as if not recognizing her voice.

"Nigga don't act like you don't recognize my voice!" she spat. "Why are you just now calling me?"

"I've been busy."

"What, you got a job?" she asked with attitude.

Mario was quiet for a few seconds. Then, he asked, "So, you found that?"

"I told you I found it, Mario," she replied, still indecisive about how she was going to handle that. She already knew she was not going to let him know where she lived. "Who does it belong to?"

"Huh?"

"Huh, hell!" she retorted, stirring the grits. "I already know you stole it from somebody."

"I ain't steal that!" he contradicted, sounding like a small child that had been caught in the act. "Why do you think I borrowed that money from you? I told you I needed to re-up."

"You said you was going in half with somebody," she reminded him. "I only gave you two hundred dollars. Now if you know somebody that got 'em for four hundred, then you need to turn me on, asap!"

He was quiet.

"You stay on Bankhead?" Shonda was ready to conclude this call.

"Yeah."

"Meet me in the parking lot of Petro, tomorrow," she told him. "Eight pm, if you're not there by eight-thirty, I'm gone. I'll be in the same truck you saw me in."

Shonda ended the call, right as Sheila entered the kitchen, still wearing the same skirt from last night, being that she was too drunk to take it off when they returned home.

"You got a date?" Sheila asked, catching the finale of Shonda's conversation.

"Nah," she answered. "That was Mario, I have to meet him tomorrow."

Sheila didn't question the configuration of the meeting. Once they'd eaten, Sheila showered while Shonda prepared the seven orders for the clients they had to meet. By the time Ebony and Theresa had shown up, accompanied by the Queenzmen, they were ready to go.

"How's Spenz doing?" Shonda asked Theresa, once inside the truck. She remembered that he was livid, last night, after making it to the finals, and losing to DJ Goldfinger.

"He called me this morning," she answered. "He's okay. He said he knew he was gonna lose because the crowd had been rooting for Goldfinger all night."

"Yeah, they had," Ebony, who was driving, concurred. "What about you, Sheila, you aight?"

"I'm good."

"You ain't seen no UFOs, have you?"

Everyone laughed, except for Sheila, who refused to entertain Ebony's teasing. Of course, she was drunk last night, but not before she'd spotted Ray. She had never heard anything about him having a twin brother. Now, she was thinking about his grave. Why weren't he and James buried side by side? Right, then, it dawned on her that the name of his tombstone was different from what she had seen on the doctor's chart when he was in the hospital. Then, his name was Ray Young, but on the tombstone, they had him as Raymond Bailey. Sheila didn't need a math teacher to help her put two and two together, King Ray was still alive!

Playa Ray

CHAPTER 23

It had been two years since the demise of James, Fred, Black, and Raymond. Still, to this day, Ray had not forgiven himself for allowing Raymond to take his place as a judge for the Battle of the DJs, because he had come down with a cold although Raymond begged him, and James insisted. It had also been two years since he'd spoken with his sister, April, who, at the time, had informed him that she was pregnant by Raymond. She was devastated by his death. Being that she had not called him back, Ray figured she was blaming him for the death of her unborn child's father, but he found out through his mother that she had undergone an abortion.

Being that the media had reported that all Kingz were deceased, Ray took that into consideration and laid low. Although he kept The Kingz' business going, working through Joe, Poppo and B.J., who had recruited other workers to perform miscellaneous jobs. Although he was maintaining a low profile, he still managed to visit the graves of James, Black, Fred, Raymond, and even Sylvia.

Earlier this year, Ray had heard about four women that had entered the drug game as The Queenz, claiming to be The Kingz widows. The fact that they were using The Kingz name to gain recognition, enraged him. Eventually, he had discovered their names, but they were vaguely unfamiliar to him. Therefore, he just let them be. He couldn't knock them for doing what they had to do to make it, but when he'd heard about the Battle of The DJs and was informed that The Queenz would be judging the event, he knew he had to be there.

"Are you sure you wanna do that?" Poppo had asked when Ray had announced his plan.

"Yeah," Ray answered. "As a matter of fact, I'm coming out of hibernation. I want them niggas to know they ain't finish the job. So, instead of looking for them, they'll come looking for *me*. May the best man win!"

Poppo didn't oppose, instead, he called Joe, and two of his affiliates to accompany them to the event. Once they got inside the club and found a spot on the back wall, Ray had forgot about The

Queenz for a moment, as he searched the crowd of DJs, looking for Spenz and Goldfinger. Once he'd spotted them, he diverted his attention to the VIP booth, where The Queenz were stationed with four men standing at the entrance like guards.

Then, almost instantly, one of The Queenz that seemed to be looking in his direction choked on her drink. He couldn't make out her features for the distance and dimness of the lights, but he couldn't say the same for her. He didn't know what she'd seen, but she abruptly got up, exited the booth, and marched through the crowd as if she was on a mission, followed by one of the guards. She was short, but he could see the sparkle of her tiara as she headed in his direction.

Before he could convey this to his guys, they formed a human fortress in front of him, indicating they were on point. Ray just dropped his head, allowing the brim of his hat to hide his face. When she approached, all he could see were her legs. He thought she would go away, seeing that she had the wrong guy, but that was not the case when she called his name, he knew, as well as she did, that she did not have the wrong guy, but Ray refused to acknowledge her. When she turned and retreated through the crowd, he knew she was going to broadcast his presence to the others. That's when he decided it was time to make a quick exit.

****

The Queenz had made their drops for the day, and returned to their homes, after dining at Ruby Tuesday's. Ebony and Theresa were watching TV in the living room when Spenz showed up a little after eight.

"I got good news, and bad news," Spenz asserted when Theresa opened the door for him. "Which one y'all wanna hear first?"

"Give us the bad news first," Ebony told him.

"The bad news is I can't spend the night," he said. "I gotta handle some business."

"Hell, that's good news to me!" said Ebony. "Now what's the other good news?"

"L.K.S. wanna meet with y'all," he announced. "This Saturday, at Grown Folks, in Roswell, eight o'clock."

"Why now?" Theresa asked, finding it odd, being that L.K.S. didn't want any dealings with them.

Spenz answered, "I don't know, I guess he's ready to deal with y'all, seeing that y'all ain't bullshitting. Maybe somebody put a word in for y'all."

Theresa didn't intend to dwell on that. She had called Spenz over for one reason, and that was to satisfy her sexual needs.

****

"You're gonna call me when you get home?" Theresa asked Spenz as they stood on the front porch.

"I'll call you tomorrow," he told her. "I told you I gotta handle some business. Ain't no telling when I'll get back to the crib."

"Okay." She kissed him in the mouth. "Drive safe, baby."

Spenz waited until Theresa had gone back inside, before climbing behind the wheel of his blue '84 Chevy Caprice on twenty-four-inch chrome wheels and pulling off. He didn't plan on having sex with Theresa, today, until she'd called him like he knew she would and insisted she was in need. Now, he had to stop by his place, first and take a quick shower, because it would be disrespectful to show up at Felicia's house smelling like another woman.

Spenz had maintained a friendship with Felicia, on the strength of Black, but they'd become closer than he thought they would. Now, he was on his way to her place to have sex with her for the first time. Something inside him was telling him not to, but Felicia wasn't the type of woman that a man would just turn down. Hell, Ru Paul wouldn't be able to resist!

Spenz pulled to a stop light at an intersection. Remembering Felicia had told him to call her when he was on his way, he pulled out his cell phone to dial her number, but before he could dial the first number, he heard the screeching of tires. He looked up to see an older model Buick had swooped in from his left side, blocking him off. Two masked men were already lunging from the front and rear passenger seats, armed with handguns.

"Get the fuck out the car!" one of them demanded when they both approached the driver's door. "Hurry the fuck up!"

Spenz had never been put in such a predicament before, but he wasn't the least bit scared. His gun was sitting in the slot of the driver's door, and he was thinking of playing on these goons intelligence by feigning to reach for the door handle, but going for his heat, instead.

"Nigga, you need to be moving!" the second goon spat.

"Okay, okay!" Spenz asserted, raising both hands, then slowly lowering his left hand as if reaching for the handle, but they were smarter than he thought.

Peeping his move, the second goon shot Spenz in the head, killing him. Once they'd pulled him out of the car, they climbed in and sped off behind the Buick, leaving Spenz in the middle of the street.

CHAPTER 24

Ray was in his back yard, feeding his two Rottweilers, when Poppo appeared in the doorway, informing him that BJ had arrived. Ray petted his dogs for a few seconds, then entered the house. B.J. and his protégé, Rick, were waiting in the living room.

"What up!" B.J. greeted him.

"I can't call it," Ray answered, hugging him and dapping Rick. "Have a seat." Once they were all seated, Ray asked. "So, what's the word?"

"We caught the nigga that ran off with that brick," B.J. announced. "We got word that he had been hiding out on Bankhead."

"And?" Ray asked, seeking confirmation.

"He won't run off with nothing else!" B.J. confirmed.

"That's what's up," Ray said, nodding.

He still couldn't believe how mature B.J. had become since T-Roc, his last protégé, was murdered in Ray's apartment on the night Fred, Black, James, and Raymond were killed. He blamed himself for leaving T-Roc at the apartment alone, so he could catch the Battle of The DJs, which was why he'd been hitting the streets hard, looking for answers.

"And we still ain't heard nothing on them, shooters," added Rick.

Ray wasn't at all surprised. He'd been getting the same results for two years, which was why he'd decided to come out of hiding. He felt that the only way to catch them was to use himself as bait, but first, he would have to stir up the water to get their attention.

Also, what he found strange, was how the Kingzmen had mysteriously disappeared after the tragic shooting. He hadn't heard anything on them, until June, when two of them were found dead on the expressway. According to the report, they were engaged in a shoot-out on the expressway, when they were both shot multiple times through the windshield of a black H-2 Hummer that they were in before it flipped over.

'*A black H-2 Hummer,*' Ray thought. The same truck that he'd seen following him on several occasions before The Kingz were murdered.

That definitely put the Kingzmen at the top of his list.

****

"He better bring his ass on!" Shonda stated, checking her watch to see that it was 8:26 pm.

The Queenz accompanied by the Queenzmen had made it to Petro on Bankhead Highway, a few minutes before eight to meet with Mario. It took Shonda a while to decide what she was going to give him but seeing that they had made a huge profit from the kilo, she settled with reimbursing him with one of theirs. What he did with it, was totally up to him.

Now, she was thinking about what Theresa said about L.K.S. wanting to meet with them. She didn't know what to make of this. They had already done business with Vincent, so they didn't need anything from him unless he was ready to provide them with answers as to who he was, and how was he connected to The Kingz. For that reason, Shonda was all for driving out to Roswell, this Saturday.

"This nigga still ain't answering!" Theresa huffed from the back seat. She'd been calling Spenz' number since eleven that morning and leaving messages to no avail.

"Calm down, baby," Shonda told her. "As soon as we leave here, we'll drive out to the club, so you can whoop his ass!"

8:35 rolled around, and Mario still hadn't shown up. Shonda gave up, she started the truck and headed for Club Strokers. It was shortly after nine when they pulled into the lot to see that neither one of Spenz' vehicles were there, but they spotted Spenz' surrogate DJ pulling his equipment from his car. Shonda pulled up on him, rolling her window down.

"Do you always get here before Spenz?" Shonda asked him, hoping that was the case.

"Nah," he answered. "I work at another club. Clyde called me, earlier, and told me the bad news. He asked me if I—"

"What bad news?" Theresa already had her window down.

"That Spenz was murdered last night."

Playa Ray

CHAPTER 25

It was Saturday, the day of Spenz' and Mario's funerals. They had found out that Mario was murdered the same night as Spenz, in an abandoned house, where junkies would go to get high or sleep. Dee and Montez told them that Mario was a junkie and had purchased drugs from them numerous times.

Being that Spenz's service was held in Atlanta, and Mario's was held in Decatur, at the same time, they attended Spenz' service with intentions to visit Mario's grave, afterward. They'd managed to get a seat on the second row, with the Queenzmen on the third. They had never met Spenz' family but assumed that they were the ones on the front row with Spenz' cousin, J-Bo, who Shonda was familiar with. Also, at the service was Clyde and some of the dancers from the club. Even Felicia who was in tears was present. Shonda still hadn't told her girls about her.

Being that Theresa had cried from the moment she'd received the news, she figured she was all cried out by now because she hadn't shed one tear, today. As she sat, watching the closed casket and listening to the Reverend speak, all she could think about was finding whoever was responsible. As she thought about both murders, she couldn't help but think someone was targeting them. Perhaps they had used Mario and Spenz as a warning.

After the service, The Queenz visited Mario's grave, then retreated to Shonda and Sheila's house to determine whether they should make the meeting with L.K.S. tonight.

"I don't think we should," said Ebony, looking around the table at her girls. "We don't know this guy. As far as we know, he could be leading us into his trap."

"Anybody agree?" Shonda asked, her mind already made.

"It's possible," Sheila answered.

"What do *you* think, Shonda?" Theresa asked. "It seems like you're on another page, right now."

"I'm going," she stated confidently. "I don't have a bad vibe about it. If y'all do stay, I'm going."

The rest of them were quiet like they were weighing their options. Shonda was hoping that they didn't try to talk her out of it because they would be wasting their breaths.

"Well, I guess we get a chance to try out our new bullet-proof vests," Sheila finally said.

"I still wish they came in pink," said Ebony.

"It's gonna take me a while to get into mine," Theresa asserted, cupping her large breast.

Shonda was happy to see that her girls despite their fears would journey to the end of the world with her, even if they knew that they would not be returning.

****

Once Ebony and Theresa had gone home, changed clothes and returned. The Queenz were en route to Roswell, with the Queenzmen in tow, arriving at the restaurant, minutes before the intended time, and leaving two Queenzmen outside.

Grown Folks was like Piccadilly, but bigger. Not to appear suspicious to the crowd while waiting for L.K.S., The Queenz went through the line, picked out a few dishes, paid for them, then found a table for five, just in case L.K.S. did intend to meet with them.

As they conversed and pretended to enjoy their food, Shonda kept an eye on Ant and Shelton, who were seated together across the room. Once the two outside spotted anyone that could pass for L.K.S., or a possible threat, they would call Ant and give him the heads up.

That call came in, shortly after eight. Ant looked over at Shonda, held up three fingers, and nodded towards the door.

"We got three coming in," Shonda said low enough to be heard only by her girls.

They all reached a hand down in their pocketbooks, keeping one hand above the table, and eyes locked on the entrance. Seconds later, two guys entered looking around. Shonda immediately recognized them as the two lieutenants she had endeavored to trail from Club Strokers. Right behind them was incontestably L.K.S. Now,

Shonda knew why she couldn't come up with a name to match the initials: It wasn't a name, but a title and the title suited him because he was definitely the *Last King Standing*.

To Be Continued…
Kingz of the Game 4
Coming Soon

Submission Guideline

Submit the first three chapters of your completed manuscript to ldpsubmissions@gmail.com, subject line: Your book's title. The manuscript must be in a .doc file and sent as an attachment. Document should be in Times New Roman, double spaced and in size 12 font. Also, provide your synopsis and full contact information. If sending multiple submissions, they must each be in a separate email.

Have a story but no way to send it electronically? You can still submit to LDP/Ca$h Presents. Send in the first three chapters, written or typed, of your completed manuscript to:

LDP: Submissions Dept
Po Box 870494
Mesquite, Tx 75187

DO NOT send original manuscript. Must be a duplicate.

Provide your synopsis and a cover letter containing your full contact information.

Thanks for considering LDP and Ca$h Presents.

BOW DOWN TO MY GANGSTA

By **Ca$h**

TORN BETWEEN TWO

By **Coffee**

BLOOD STAINS OF A SHOTTA **III**

By **Jamaica**

STEADY MOBBIN **III**

By **Marcellus Allen**

BLOOD OF A BOSS **VI**

By **Askari**

LOYAL TO THE GAME **IV**

LIFE OF SIN **III**

By **T.J. & Jelissa**

A DOPEBOY'S PRAYER **II**

By **Eddie "Wolf" Lee**

IF LOVING YOU IS WRONG… **III**

By **Jelissa**

TRUE SAVAGE **VII**

By **Chris Green**

BLAST FOR ME **III**

DUFFLE BAG CARTEL **IV**

By **Ghost**

ADDICTIED TO THE DRAMA **III**

By **Jamila Mathis**

A HUSTLER'S DECEIT 3

KILL ZONE **II**

BAE BELONGS TO ME III

SOUL OF A MONSTER II

By **Aryanna**

THE COST OF LOYALTY **III**

By **Kweli**

SHE FELL IN LOVE WITH A REAL ONE **II**

By **Tamara Butler**

RENEGADE BOYS **III**

By **Meesha**

A GANGSTER'S SYN II

By **J-Blunt**

KING OF NEW YORK V

RISE TO POWER III

COKE KINGS III

By **T.J. Edwards**

GORILLAZ IN THE BAY IV

De'Kari

THE STREETS ARE CALLING II

Duquie Wilson

KINGPIN KILLAZ IV

STREET KINGS 2

PAID IN BLOOD 2

Hood Rich

SINS OF A HUSTLA II

ASAD

TRIGGADALE III

Elijah R. Freeman

MARRIED TO A BOSS III

By **Destiny Skai & Chris Green**

KINGZ OF THE GAME IV

Playa Ray

SLAUGHTER GANG III

By **Willie Slaughter**
THE HEART OF A SAVAGE II
By **Jibril Williams**
FUK SHYT II
By **Blakk Diamond**
THE DOPEMAN'S BODYGAURD II
By **Tranay Adams**

<u>Available Now</u>
<u>RESTRAINING ORDER **I & II**</u>
By **CA$H & Coffee**
<u>LOVE KNOWS NO BOUNDARIES **I II & III**</u>
By **Coffee**
<u>RAISED AS A GOON I, II, III & IV</u>
<u>BRED BY THE SLUMS I, II, III</u>
<u>BLAST FOR ME I & II</u>
<u>ROTTEN TO THE CORE I II III</u>
<u>A BRONX TALE I, II, III</u>
<u>DUFFEL BAG CARTEL I II III</u>
By **Ghost**
<u>LAY IT DOWN **I & II**</u>
<u>LAST OF A DYING BREED</u>
<u>BLOOD STAINS OF A SHOTTA I & II</u>
By **Jamaica**
<u>LOYAL TO THE GAME</u>
<u>LOYAL TO THE GAME II</u>
<u>LOYAL TO THE GAME III</u>
<u>LIFE OF SIN I, II</u>

Playa Ray

By **TJ & Jelissa**
BLOODY COMMAS I & II
SKI MASK CARTEL I II & III
KING OF NEW YORK I II,III IV
RISE TO POWER I II
COKE KINGS I II
By **T.J. Edwards**
IF LOVING HIM IS WRONG…I & II
LOVE ME EVEN WHEN IT HURTS I II III
By **Jelissa**
WHEN THE STREETS CLAP BACK I & II III
By **Jibril Williams**
A DISTINGUISHED THUG STOLE MY HEART I II & III
LOVE SHOULDN'T HURT I II III IV
RENEGADE BOYS I & II
By **Meesha**
A GANGSTER'S CODE I &, II III
A GANGSTER'S SYN
By J-Blunt
PUSH IT TO THE LIMIT
By **Bre' Hayes**
BLOOD OF A BOSS **I, II, III, IV, V**
By **Askari**
THE STREETS BLEED MURDER **I, II & III**
THE HEART OF A GANGSTA I II& III
By **Jerry Jackson**
CUM FOR ME
CUM FOR ME 2
CUM FOR ME 3
CUM FOR ME 4

230

CUM FOR ME 5

An **LDP Erotica Collaboration**

BRIDE OF A HUSTLA **I II & II**

THE FETTI GIRLS **I, II& III**

CORRUPTED BY A GANGSTA I, II III, IV

By **Destiny Skai**

WHEN A GOOD GIRL GOES BAD

By **Adrienne**

THE COST OF LOYALTY

By Kweli

A GANGSTER'S REVENGE **I II III & IV**

THE BOSS MAN'S DAUGHTERS

THE BOSS MAN'S DAUGHTERS II

THE BOSSMAN'S DAUGHTERS III

THE BOSSMAN'S DAUGHTERS IV

THE BOSS MAN'S DAUGHTERS **V**

A SAVAGE LOVE **I & II**

BAE BELONGS TO ME I II

A HUSTLER'S DECEIT I, II, III

WHAT BAD BITCHES DO I, II, III

SOUL OF A MONSTER

By **Aryanna**

A KINGPIN'S AMBITON

A KINGPIN'S AMBITION **II**

I MURDER FOR THE DOUGH

By **Ambitious**

TRUE SAVAGE

TRUE SAVAGE II

TRUE SAVAGE **III**

TRUE SAVAGE **IV**

Playa Ray

TRUE SAVAGE **V**

TRUE SAVAGE **VI**

By **Chris Green**

A DOPEBOY'S PRAYER

By **Eddie "Wolf" Lee**

THE KING CARTEL **I, II & III**

By **Frank Gresham**

THESE NIGGAS AIN'T LOYAL **I, II & III**

By **Nikki Tee**

GANGSTA SHYT **I II &III**

By **CATO**

THE ULTIMATE BETRAYAL

By **Phoenix**

BOSS'N UP **I , II & III**

By **Royal Nicole**

I LOVE YOU TO DEATH

By Destiny J

I RIDE FOR MY HITTA

I STILL RIDE FOR MY HITTA

By **Misty Holt**

LOVE & CHASIN' PAPER

By **Qay Crockett**

TO DIE IN VAIN

SINS OF A HUSTLA

By **ASAD**

BROOKLYN HUSTLAZ

By **Boogsy Morina**

BROOKLYN ON LOCK I & II

By **Sonovia**

GANGSTA CITY

By **Teddy Duke**

A DRUG KING AND HIS DIAMOND I & II III

A DOPEMAN'S RICHES

HER MAN, MINE'S TOO I, II

CASH MONEY HO'S

By **Nicole Goosby**

TRAPHOUSE KING **I II & III**

KINGPIN KILLAZ I II III

STREET KINGS

PAID IN BLOOD

By **Hood Rich**

LIPSTICK KILLAH **I, II, III**

CRIME OF PASSION I & II

By **Mimi**

STEADY MOBBN' **I, II, III**

By **Marcellus Allen**

WHO SHOT YA **I, II, III**

Renta

GORILLAZ IN THE BAY **I II III**

DE'KARI

TRIGGADALE I II

Elijah R. Freeman

GOD BLESS THE TRAPPERS I, II, III

THESE SCANDALOUS STREETS I, II, III

FEAR MY GANGSTA I, II, III

THESE STREETS DON'T LOVE NOBODY I, II

BURY ME A G I, II, III, IV, V

A GANGSTA'S EMPIRE I, II, III, IV

THE DOPEMAN'S BODYGAURD

Tranay Adams

Playa Ray

THE STREETS ARE CALLING
Duquie Wilson
MARRIED TO A BOSS... I II
By Destiny Skai & Chris Green
KINGZ OF THE GAME I II III
Playa Ray
SLAUGHTER GANG I II
By Willie Slaughter
THE HEART OF A SAVAGE
By Jibril Williams
FUK SHYT
By Blakk Diamond

BOOKS BY LDP'S CEO, CA$H

TRUST IN NO MAN

TRUST IN NO MAN 2

TRUST IN NO MAN 3

BONDED BY BLOOD

SHORTY GOT A THUG

THUGS CRY

THUGS CRY 2

THUGS CRY 3

TRUST NO BITCH

TRUST NO BITCH 2

TRUST NO BITCH 3

TIL MY CASKET DROPS

RESTRAINING ORDER

RESTRAINING ORDER 2

IN LOVE WITH A CONVICT

Coming Soon

BONDED BY BLOOD 2

BOW DOWN TO MY GANGSTA

Playa Ray